SOLO

Nurse Melissa Warren suspects something has to be
very wrong in surgeon Ben Gregory's life. But considering she doesn't even like him he appears to be
taking up far more of her attention than he deserves!

First published in Great Britain 1983
by Mills & Boon Limited, 15–16 Brook's Mews,
London W1A 1DR

© Lynne Collins 1983

Australian copyright 1983
Philippine copyright 1983

ISBN 0 263 74480 9

Set in 10 on 12 pt Linotron Times
03/1183

Photoset by Rowland Phototypesetting Ltd
Bury St Edmunds, Suffolk
Made and printed in Great Britain by
Richard Clay (The Chaucer Press) Ltd
Bungay, Suffolk

SOLO SURGEON

BY

LYNNE COLLINS

MILLS & BOON LIMITED
London · Sydney · Toronto

CHAPTER ONE

MELISSA came out of Matron's office, smiling. She had been offered an extension to her contract as a theatre nurse at St Biddulph's and she was delighted. She enjoyed working in Theatres and she had been very happy during the past six months.

At first she had felt a few doubts about leaving Hartlake, her training hospital in London where she had been a staff nurse for two years, but she had decided that she was due for a change. Five years in one hospital was enough for any girl unless she had ambitions to be a ward sister, she felt. St Biddulph's had offered just the right opportunity at just the right time. She liked Norfolk, having happy memories of family holidays there in the past. An aunt and some cousins still lived within twenty miles of Baymouth and as they were all the family she had left, it had been an added inducement to apply for a job at the town's new hospital.

Six months later, she was glad to renew her contract and she crossed the bustling main hall with a light step and a smile for everyone that she passed. Meeting a friend, she stopped to tell her the good news.

Vicki had started at St Biddulph's on the same day as herself and they had liked each other on sight. Being a local girl, she had been helpful in finding Melissa a small flat that was reasonably close to the hospital at a rent she could comfortably afford. She had introduced her to people and places and generally proved to be a good friend.

Now she was just as pleased as Melissa. 'That's marvellous!' she declared warmly. 'Not that I doubted the outcome for a moment, of course. You're an asset to this place and they wouldn't want to lose you. Besides, I hear that almost every male member of staff signed a petition for you to stay. Apparently you brighten their overworked lives.'

Melissa laughed. 'Idiot! Very few male members of staff even know I exist!'

'You'd be surprised. You're much too modest,' Vicki told her lightly. 'But this calls for a celebration! I'm off duty until three and I'll treat you to a glass of shandy and a ham sandwich at the Jubilee. Unless you've other plans?'

'You've just made me an offer I can't refuse,' Melissa agreed, amused.

The two girls reached the main entrance just as a tall and strikingly handsome man thrust his way through the door and forcefully collided with the slightly-built Melissa. He was obviously in a tearing hurry. He also seemed to be in a foul mood. He glowered at her as though she was to blame for being in his way, muttered something that might or might not have been an apology, and strode on his way.

Melissa looked after him, gingerly rubbing a near-dislocated shoulder. Tall and broad and very powerful, he had probably been a useful rugger player in his medical student days, she thought dryly.

Winded and rather annoyed by his brusque manner, she said sharply, 'That man is so blinded by conceit that he can't seem to see anything else!'

Vicki looked at her, a little surprised. It wasn't like the sweet-natured Melissa to react so tartly to an accidental encounter. 'Something seems to have upset our new SSO,' she drawled. '*Is* he so conceited? He's certainly attractive. Quite devastating . . .' She turned to look after the rapidly retreating surgeon with admiring eyes.

'Dangerous, you mean!' Melissa passed through the door and emerged into the bright sunshine of the June day. 'In every sense of the word, I should think.'

'Really . . . ?'

Hearing the quickening interest in her friend's tone, Melissa wished she hadn't uttered those dry words. She had learned that Vicki was a romantic, easily impressed, and much too likely to fall lightly into love without looking beyond a man's physical attributes.

She was flirtatious and fickle but it was all very light-hearted and entirely innocent. Pretty and popular and personable, she had been in and out of love so many times in the last six months that Melissa had lost count. Now, being briefly between boyfriends, it seemed that Vicki had decided to recognise that the fairly new addition to the staff of St Biddulph's was a very attractive man.

Melissa wasn't impressed, although he did have more than his fair share of good looks with that fine, bronze head and those deep-set grey eyes and lean, handsome face. She had never fallen into the trap of judging anyone by appearance.

Being a practical, level-headed girl, with her feet firmly on the ground, she didn't give her affections easily and she kept friendship with the opposite sex on a strictly platonic basis. She felt that one day she would meet someone that she could love with all her heart and want to marry, and she didn't want a long string of foolish affairs to her credit in the meantime.

So she didn't share the general excitement and speculation about Ben Gregory for all his good looks, or the fact that he was a very eligible bachelor. She was much more interested in his surgical skill, his attitude to his colleagues, his caring concern for his patients and the fact that he had a rather unorthodox approach to certain cases.

As a man, she wasn't sure that she liked him, but he was a very good surgeon and she admired and respected his work in Theatres. She enjoyed working with him very much and she could overlook the cool arrogance of his attitude outside Theatres.

'Are you all right?' Vicki suddenly remembered to be solicitous.

'I'll survive.' Melissa smiled at her friend as they walked towards the gates and the main road. 'I'm sorry it was me,' she teased. 'I expect you feel it would have been worth a few bruises to have him bump into you!'

Vicki grinned. 'I'd have worn a sling for a few days so he knew me again! That's for sure!'

'I don't think he saw either of us,' Melissa declared. 'He had far too much on his mind to know that he'd bumped into anyone—least of all a mere nurse!'

Fleetingly, she wondered if he was anxious about that emergency appendicectomy—there had been acute peritoneal infection and the boy was low—or if he had personal problems.

Women trouble, perhaps, she thought with a flicker of

amusement as she listened with only half an ear to Vicki's account of her busy morning on Men's Surgical while she sat with her friend in the warm sunshine of the pub garden that was popular with the hospital staff when they were off duty.

With those looks, it would be rather surprising if there weren't lots of women in Ben Gregory's life, most of them trying to lure him to the altar. For doctors were always fair game for husband hunters and several nurses were known to have been casting out lures ever since he had arrived at St Biddulph's to take up his appointment as Senior Surgical Officer.

Because of her particular job, Melissa saw more of him than most of her fellow-nurses but her conscience was clear. She didn't think they'd exchanged two words outside the operating theatre in the past three weeks. She knew he hadn't recognised her that morning even if he'd had time to spare a glance for the girl who got in his way.

She was just a theatre nurse, an efficient pair of hands attached to a green surgical gown, a pair of dark blue eyes above a green surgical mask that watched his every move and anticipated his every need while those strong, skilful hands went about their very important work. Wearing her own clothes because she was off duty and with her ash-blonde hair framing her face instead of being tucked clinically out of sight beneath the theatre mob cap, she must have been quite unrecognisable, she thought, dryly amused.

'He isn't married, is he?'

Vicki's question broke into her reverie. Melissa looked at her rather blankly. 'Who . . . ?'

'Our Mr Gregory, of course! Haven't you been listening? I've been talking about him for ten minutes,' Vicki said reproachfully.

'Sorry. I was day-dreaming.' Melissa smiled an apology.

'Obviously not about our good-looking SSO! Or you'd have been hanging on my every word since I mentioned his name! I was just wondering why he doesn't take up any of the offers he's had since he came here. He isn't married, is he?'

'No. Someone said that he's engaged to a nurse at a hospital in Bury St Edmunds. I don't know if it's true. You know as well as I do that grapevine gossip isn't at all reliable.'

'Well, he *ought* to be married,' Vicki averred, mock indignant. 'Leaving a dream like that loose to flutter all our hearts and raise our hopes just isn't fair!'

Melissa laughed. 'He doesn't flutter *my* heart!'

'I believe you. But thousands wouldn't,' Vicki teased. 'It just isn't natural. Just think of all your opportunities, too!'

'And in such romantic surroundings,' she returned dryly. '"Scalpel, please, Nurse—and how about dinner tonight? Wipe my brow, please—and come out for a drink this evening. Needle and catgut—and are you fainting at the sight of blood or is it the effect of my big blue eyes, Nurse?"'

'Oh, so you've noticed his blue eyes?' Vicki demanded promptly. 'Shame on you, Nurse Warren!'

'They aren't blue, as a matter of fact. They're grey, just like flint, and equally as hard,' Melissa told her lightly. 'I can't help noticing when they meet mine all the time over the operating table—and heaven help me if I'm not quick enough to know what's wanted without being told! He has the most unsmiling eyes I've ever met!'

'You really don't like him, do you?' Vicki was curious.

Melissa shrugged. 'Not particularly—and he isn't interested in being liked, Vicki. All he wants is an efficient robot that he can safely ignore outside the operating theatre without any risk of reproach.' As she spoke, she realised that she was still smarting slightly from that brief and painful encounter with the surgeon—and she wasn't thinking of her shoulder. She was rather surprised that his curt indifference should rankle.

'I thought the atmosphere in Theatres was so friendly,' Vicki said slowly.

'So it is. He isn't *un*friendly. Just impersonal. He's dedicated to his work and doesn't waste time or energy on frivolities like conversation or smiling,' she said dryly.

'The strong, silent type?'

'Until something annoys him. Then he isn't so silent. You should have heard him wiping the floor with Jamie Greaves the other day. You know what *he's* like. Plays the fool to ease the first tensions of the day. Well, it didn't go down at all well with our Mr Gregory, I'm afraid. It was the first time they'd worked together. The atmosphere was decidedly strained until the SSO realised that Jamie was really good at his job for all the clowning. He said as much, Jamie apologised, and all was well!'

Vicki looked at her thoughtfully. 'You know, he really sounds the down to earth, no-nonsense, straight from the shoulder type that you *ought* to like, Melissa. Some-one just like yourself!'

'Heavens!' she exclaimed in laughing protest. 'I think I'm meant to be flattered. Instead, I feel *flattened*! What a dreadful description! Inside, I'm all fluttery and femi-nine, a little woman looking for a big strong man to take care of me—and now you tell me that everyone sees me as the tweed skirts, brogues and shooting-stick type with no time for men! Oh, well, truth will out! No wonder I haven't any boyfriends!'

'You could have dozens if you weren't so busily keeping them all at bay,' Vicki told her with truth. 'I don't know why you can't relax and have some fun like everyone else. You can't want to end up an old maid. Or worse!' she added darkly.

Melissa raised an amused eyebrow. 'I wonder what could be worse? Marriage to someone like Ben Gregory, I suppose,' she added, mock innocent. 'Relaxing and having fun doesn't seem much in his line, either.'

'I do see what you mean,' Vicki said softly, with a nudge of her elbow and a jerk of her dark head at the tall man who had just appeared in the pub doorway and was surveying the sunny garden with a frown in his eyes.

His glance skated across them with utter indifference. He began to make his way towards a vacant seat in the shade, carrying a tankard of ice-cold beer. He looked very stern and forbidding despite those good looks, but it took a lot to repress the pretty and light-hearted Vicki who was used to being noticed rather than ignored by men.

'Good afternoon, Mr Gregory!' she chirruped lightly as he reached them.

He turned his head at the sound of his name. But Melissa wondered if those bleak eyes even saw her pretty friend.

'Yes,' he said absently, unsmiling.

Vicki's bright smile almost faded, but she wasn't easily snubbed. 'Do join us,' she invited, moving to make room for him on the wooden bench. 'I wanted to ask you something about Mrs Withers on my ward and I've missed your round.'

Melissa thought he looked at them both with dislike and certainly with a hint of annoyance.

'Not just now, Nurse,' he said curtly. '*Off duty* means exactly that in my book.' And he walked on.

Two bright spots of anger stained Vicki's cheeks at the rebuff. 'Now I know why you don't like him, Melissa,' she said, loudly enough for him to hear.

Melissa knew that he had heard. She saw the stiffening of that broad back, the tensing of the proud head. It wouldn't have mattered if she didn't have the kind of name that wasn't at all usual. She might be a very rigid Nurse Warren to him but she was an informal Melissa to everyone else in Theatres and he must have abruptly realised her identity as Vicki's light voice carried across the garden.

As he sat down and put his beer on the wooden table, he glanced towards Melissa and their eyes met briefly. His grey eyes narrowed sharply as though he admitted to recognising her now and she glanced away, slightly embarrassed by the echo of Vicki's scornful words. She had no wish to seem interested in someone so obviously indifferent to her as a person. She *wasn't* interested. She didn't like him very much and she was quite content to keep their relationship within the impersonal confines of the operating theatre, she decided proudly.

Rather disconcerted by her friend's reaction which had involved her so summarily, she would have liked to get up and go. But she couldn't think of an excuse that would convince Vicki and she certainly didn't want her or Ben Gregory to suppose that his off-hand attitude had driven her away.

Vicki was able to dismiss the incident with ease and seemed content to sit in the sun and talk shop until it was time for her to return to her ward. Determined that the surgeon's presence in the pub garden shouldn't make a scrap of difference to her enjoyment of the golden weather and Vicki's company, Melissa proceeded to ignore him.

But she couldn't help noticing that he didn't seem to be enjoying his beer or his break from the day's demands or his own company. The glass stood almost untouched on the table while he leaned forward with hands locked together between his knees, staring at the ground.

Melissa saw that a nerve throbbed in his lean cheek. He looked tense and a little angry and, occasionally, rather unhappy. It seemed that his private thoughts weren't providing him with the least pleasure or satisfaction.

Being a warm-hearted, sensitive girl with the kind of caring and compassionate nature that had originally taken her into nursing, she didn't like to feel that he was depressed or anxious even if she didn't like him very much.

Vicki went into the pub for a packet of crisps. Left alone, Melissa sat irresolute for a few moments, her gaze on the silently brooding surgeon. Then, on an impulse that she regretted even before she reached him, she rose and crossed the strip of lawn to where he sat. He wasn't immediately aware of her approach, he was too preoccupied with his thoughts.

'Excuse me . . . Mr Gregory?' It was quiet, slightly hesitant.

He glanced up quickly, guarded. 'Well?'

It wasn't encouraging. Impulse had carried her this far, but before the obvious coolness of his grey eyes and his voice, concern ebbed away and she merely felt that she was intruding. 'I just wondered—if there was anything wrong?' It came out lamely, sounding like idle and impertinent curiosity instead of well-meant sympathy.

His eyes narrowed with suspicion. 'Nothing that concerns you,' he said coldly.

Her face flamed. 'How could it?' she retorted with a touch of spirit. 'It's obviously a personal matter!' A growing dislike of his impersonality and resentment of his refusal to offer or accept the slightest overture of friendship, coloured her impulsive and rather tart words.

'Very personal,' he agreed brusquely.

Melissa turned away, raging inside at his rebuffing manner and her own stupidity in approaching him at all. She found that she was trembling and felt slightly sick with dismay that she had not only invited but been handed such an unmistakable snub.

He saw something of her feelings in the shadow that crossed her expressive face. 'Just a minute, Nurse Warren. I don't mean to be rude, you know,' he said harshly.

'But you chose the wrong moment to take an interest in my affairs.'

She looked at him coldly. 'Please don't run away with the idea that I have the slightest interest in your affairs— or in *you*, Mr Gregory!' Ice tinkled in her tone.

'Then what the devil brought you over here with your damn fool questions?' he demanded.

'I wish I knew!' she retorted angrily. 'It was certainly a mistake!'

She left him with as much dignity as she could muster and hurried to intercept Vicki who was on her way back with the crisps.

'Sorry to rush away,' she said as lightly as if there wasn't a tempest raging within her breast. 'But I've just remembered that I promised to visit Aunt Eleanor this afternoon and I should just make the two o'clock bus . . .'

Having met a houseman at the bar who had offered to buy her a drink, Vicki didn't mind at all—and it didn't occur to her to link Melissa's sudden departure with the surgeon who had got to his feet and was looking towards them with a frown and a slight air of uncertainty.

Melissa had just missed the bus by the time she hurried along the road to the nearest stop. She resigned herself to a twenty minute wait in the hot sun and resolved to call the little garage in town to hurry up the repair of her small and rather shabby car. At times like these, it was greatly missed.

The sudden squall of her encounter with Ben Gregory seemed to have swept all the pleasure from her day and she wondered if she really wanted to stay at St Biddulph's after all. Working with someone like the arrogant, cold-blooded and very unfriendly surgeon gave no promise of enjoyment, she thought crossly. She was shocked to discover that he could be so nasty. He had always been aloof, getting on with the work in hand without wasting time on personalities, just as she had told Vicki. But he had been civil enough.

She doubted if she would make Maresby and her aunt's garden centre that afternoon. It had just been an excuse to satisfy Vicki. Twenty miles by bus on a hot day didn't really appeal and there was plenty to do in the flat, and Aunt Eleanor wasn't expecting her.

Idly she watched the approach of a white Mercedes with a personalised number plate of BG 1 but didn't look at the driver until the car slowed and halted within a few feet of her. Ben Gregory leaned across and spoke through the open passenger window.

'I'm going into town. Do you want a lift?'

Melissa was surprised. She was also still angry. She shook her head. 'I'll wait for the bus, thanks.'

'Well, if you won't allow me to make amends . . .' He shrugged.

She looked at him doubtfully. He didn't *look* sorry. He didn't look the type to admit to a fault let alone apologise for it. He looked and sounded and seemed utterly indifferent to her tart refusal of his unexpected offer.

He had been rude and unpleasant. Perhaps it came easily to him—but perhaps it had only been prompted by circumstances and the mood of the moment, she thought charitably. A man with something weighing heavily on his mind didn't always feel like being polite or plea⸀ ⸀ to someone he didn't know very well.

Melissa didn't like to be at odds with anyone and her warm heart was swift to make allowances even though she didn't like him very much. They had to work together, too, she reminded herself. It was important that there shouldn't be friction between members of staff in Theatres. It wasn't always easy to forget personal grievances with the donning of mask and gown but when lives were at stake it was vital that a certain rapport should exist between a surgeon and his theatre nurse.

Since Ben Gregory's arrival they had worked together as a good team. He was not a man to praise and he was quick to criticise but she had felt that her work met his exacting requirements. As a Hartlake nurse, she had been well-trained and well-taught, and she was always conscious of how much was expected from any nurse who wore the distinctive silver badge of the famous teaching hospital with its world-wide reputation.

'I'm afraid that wasn't very gracious,' she said carefully. 'May I change my mind?' She smiled at him. It wasn't much of a smile but as it didn't meet with the slightest response she was glad that she hadn't wasted too much warmth on him.

He opened the car door. 'Get in.' His manner wasn't inviting and Melissa hesitated. 'Come on!' he said tersely. 'Before I change *my* mind!'

CHAPTER TWO

THE CAR shot away from the bus stop at such speed that Melissa wondered if he already regretted his quixotic impulse and couldn't wait to reach the town and be rid of her. The Mercedes seemed to consume the five miles of coast road between St Biddulph's and Baymouth town centre in no time at all.

She stole a glance at the surgeon. His strong, capable hands were as steady on the wheel as they were when wielding a scalpel or clamping an artery or delicately manoeuvring needle and nylon thread after surgery. He *was* good-looking, she conceded levelly, and he couldn't help but know it when so many silly girls were forever throwing themselves at his head.

She suddenly went cold. Surely he hadn't suspected her of the same thing when she crossed the pub garden to speak to him, solely moved by friendly concern. He had certainly snubbed her mercilessly! Just as if she was a stranger pushing herself to the notice of a man who was very attractive to women, she thought wryly—and perhaps that was exactly how he had viewed her approach.

For even after three weeks of working together under the arc lights of the operating theatre in that peculiarly close and intimate relationship of surgeon and nurse, with the single purpose of healing by the knife, she was still a stranger in his eyes, she knew.

Sensing her glance, he turned his head to look at her enquiringly. 'Sorry . . . ?'

'I didn't speak,' Melissa returned, rather stiffly. She thought dryly that if she had been talking non-stop since she got into his car, he wouldn't have known. Whatever was on his mind seemed to be excluding everything else from his notice.

'Afraid you'll get your head bitten off again, I expect.' He didn't smile but there was a flicker of ironic amusement in the grey eyes. 'Do you want the town centre, Nurse Warren?'

The formality was pointed. She wondered if he thought she might take advantage of a casual favour and interpret it as a friendly gesture. She felt like reassuring him but bit back the tart words.

'No. I'm going home, actually,' she told him instead. 'Not as far as the town. Perhaps you'd drop me at the first turning past the next roundabout. Chelmer Avenue.'

'That's where you live, is it?'

'Yes.'

He nodded. 'Not too far from the hospital. It isn't a bad journey by bus, I suppose? Is it a reliable service?'

'Pretty reliable. I don't use it very often.' He was making conversation and she wondered why he bothered when it was obviously a strain for him to be civil. 'My car has suspension trouble and is in for repair. This will do nicely,' she added hastily as she noted the flashing indicator. 'Don't come out of your way . . .'

'No trouble.' He turned left into the tree-lined avenue. 'What number?'

'Thirty-nine.' She indicated the large and rambling

Victorian mansion that had been converted into flats by a local builder. The car drew up outside the house. 'Thanks very much,' she said, rather coolly.

She had a little difficulty with the stiff door handle. He leaned across to take over and she drew back slightly from his oddly disturbing nearness. His arm brushed against her breast in the thin silk blouse. He didn't seem to notice, but that careless contact set her tingling. She smelt the rather pleasant tang of his after-shave and observed in a detached fashion that the bright sun found glints of gold among the bronze hair, worn rather long and tending to curl on the nape of his neck. She thought that his mouth would be sensual if he allowed it to relax from those grim lines. Reserved to the point of austerity, aloof and unsmiling, he was still a very attractive man . . .

'I didn't realise that you were blonde,' he said abruptly as he straightened.

'What . . . ?' Melissa was startled by the unexpected and almost accusing words.

'Your hair. It's always hidden by your theatre cap. I imagined that you were dark haired,' he explained.

'Oh!' She was puzzled and astonished to discover that he had given any thought at all to her colouring.

'I didn't recognise you immediately,' he added with a hint of impatience.

'Oh, I see.' Melissa suddenly knew that this was as near as he would get to an apology. She smiled at him, rather more warmly. 'I did know that,' she admitted.

'It wouldn't have made any difference if I had, of course,' he said bluntly. 'I didn't feel like talking to anyone at that particular moment.'

'That was obvious,' she returned dryly. She pushed the door open and moved to get out of the car. Then she paused, turning to look at him. 'I'm *not* interfering and I'm *not* prying,' she told him firmly. 'But I feel that you must have had some bad news.'

'That depends on how one looks at it,' he said brusquely. 'My friends will probably tell me that it's the very best of news—and maybe in time I shall be able to accept that they're right. Just now, it feels like very bad news to me.'

He obviously didn't mean to tell her more than that and Melissa wasn't curious. She was just concerned. That stony expression and the curt tone concealed a great deal of hurt, she felt.

'I'm sorry,' she said quietly.

His eyes narrowed. 'I believe you are, too. Why the devil should you care?' He looked at her steadily. 'You don't even like me. Do you?'

She had been careful not to let it show in their weeks of working together, so he could only have heard Vicki's words, just as she had suspected.

Meeting the grey eyes, she felt that they held a challenge. Well, if they were playing the truth game, she could be as blunt as Ben Gregory, she thought, slightly on the defensive.

'Not particularly,' she agreed lightly. 'You don't try to be liked.'

He stiffened. 'Should I?'

She shrugged. 'It greases the wheels.'

He frowned. 'If the pursuit of liking involves cuddling nurses and fulsome flattery and being heartily jolly about my work then *no*! I *don't* try to be liked!'

'A smile and a friendly word doesn't cost anything and it makes for good working relationships.'

'A smile and a friendly word can cause a great deal of trouble in my experience,' he said grimly. 'I've learned to keep a low profile, especially when impressionable young nurses are thrown a great deal into my company!'

Melissa stared at him, astonished. Then she rallied. 'Well, I'm neither very young nor at all impressionable, and I promise you that an occasional smile or a remark that isn't connected with work won't make *me* weak at the knees,' she said tartly. 'But it will make me feel less apprehensive. I seem to spend most of my time in Theatres wondering what I've done wrong or how I've offended, and I find it very uncomfortable. Working with you is like standing on the edge of a volcano!'

'I'm not likely to change the habits of a lifetime to make *you* more comfortable, Nurse Warren,' he told her, very dry.

She glanced at him quickly and wondered if she only imagined that faint glimmer of unexpected laughter in the grey eyes. It was gone in an instant and she decided that it had never been there. He was so obviously a long way from laughing at anything at this particular time. It must have been *very* bad news, she decided . . . and he couldn't want to sit in his car bandying words with her. She, too, had much better things to do with her time than waste it on a man she didn't even like!

'Thanks for the lift,' she said again with a little finality in her voice as she got out of the car.

With a cursory wave, he drove off and Melissa resolutely refused to stand at the gate, looking after the car. She knew she was already dismissed from his mind—she doubted if he was even looking in the rear mirror. But she was determined that he shouldn't have the least reason to suppose that she was interested in him or liked him more than she meant to admit. She wasn't— and she didn't!

She let herself into the flat, tucked into a corner of the ground floor of the old house. She suspected that it had once been the servants' quarters. The front door opened directly into a small sitting-room and a smaller bedroom led from it. There was a tiny kitchen and a minuscule bathroom. It suited her very well and it was cheap. The furniture was old and shabby but she had brightened the place with her own pictures and ornaments, some cheerful cushions and curtains, and it was spotlessly clean. A nurse's training had taught her to scrub and polish if nothing else, she often declared, tackling the necessary cleaning with a will. She had been busy in the flat that morning, making the most of a free day, before she caught the bus for her interview with Matron. Everything gleamed in very satisfactory manner.

Melissa made tea and curled up on the sofa to drink it, reviewing Matron's compliments on her work and the flattering assurance that an efficient theatre nurse like herself was an asset to St Biddulph's. She had gained a lot of satisfaction from work well done during the past six months and she knew that she was a good theatre nurse. That wasn't conceit but a level-headed awareness of ability that came from an excellent training and a real love of theatre work. She was also familiar with most procedures after a year in Theatres at Hartlake, working with some of the best surgeons in the world.

She wondered idly where Ben Gregory had qualified,

first in medicine and later as a Bachelor of Surgery. He wasn't a Hartlake man. He *was* a very good surgeon, a pleasure to watch and to assist, with his skill, his economy of movement and his sure hands. She wasn't decrying St Biddulph's by any means but she did wonder why he had chosen to work in a provincial hospital when he might have become a Professor of Surgery at a teaching hospital in London in due course. He might not be ambitious, of course. But she was sure that he was dedicated.

She recalled what he had said about impressionable young nurses and wondered if they had given him a great deal of trouble at other hospitals where he had worked. He *was* very good-looking even if he didn't know how to smile, she decided lightly.

Unbidden, she suddenly remembered that odd reaction to the fleeting pressure of his arm against her body. For the first time in her life she had actually tingled with an excitement that was certainly sexual, she admitted candidly, rather disturbed. Yet she had been kissed with ardour by men she liked and had even submitted to the fondling of her breasts on occasion without once experiencing that sensual stirring in the secret places of her body.

She was twenty-three and a virgin. Now she wondered if that was due to lack of temptation rather than the strict morality of her upbringing. After all, she had never been kissed and caressed by a man with the potent physical attraction of a Ben Gregory, she thought dryly.

It was something of a shock to discover that liking and affection weren't necessary to trigger that shaft of desire. It was just as well that the too-attractive surgeon was never likely to make love to her for she might not find it too easy to say no to him. No had always been firmly uttered in the past.

Her thoughts still revolving unaccountably about Ben Gregory, Melissa froze at the sound of the doorbell. Then she smiled at the absurd idea that it could be the surgeon. Why on earth would he come back, anyway?

She got up from the sofa, went to the door and opened it to her cousin Neville. Tall and blond and easy-going, he smiled down at her, confident of a welcome.

He *was* welcome, too. She was very fond of Neville. Six years older than her, he had always been tolerant of the little girl who had tagged along with him and his friends, declaring that she could climb trees and dig tunnels, could run and jump and play cricket and football like any boy. She had proved that she could, too. In her teens, she had turned from cheerful tomboy into a pretty, feminine young woman who was inclined to be shy and self-conscious in the company of her mature cousin with his string of girlfriends. Now, having seen a lot of Neville since she had come to Baymouth, she was no longer shy or self-conscious but he still had his string of girlfriends. She was always delighted when he found time to take her to the cinema or the theatre, or out dancing or arriving unexpectedly to whisk her off for a drive, or a couple of hours on the beach or to take her back to his home for the day.

She drew him in. 'How nice to see you, Neville! Sit down! There's tea in the pot. I'll just get another cup . . .'

'Not for me, thanks.'

'A lager? I've some cans in the fridge.' She hurried

into the kitchen and came back with the beer. 'Have you had lunch? I can make you a sandwich?'

He caught her wrist and drew her down onto the sofa by his side. 'I've had lunch. Stop fussing and tell me how things went at your interview.'

She was warmed that he cared enough to remember. She was never quite sure just how Neville felt about her. He seemed to hold her in more than cousinly affection at times. At other times, he was as casual as though they were brother and sister. She wasn't sure how she felt about him, either. She knew she was fond of him. She knew that she enjoyed his company. Even at sixteen and as romantic as any other girl of that age, she had never fancied herself in love with her good-looking cousin. At twenty-three she was still reluctant to think of him in that light. But she did like him more than any other man she knew and secretly she was rather glad that not one of his many girlfriends had yet managed to marry him.

Neville didn't want to settle down. He liked his freedom and he was something of a playboy. He had plenty of money and he enjoyed spending it on fast cars and pretty girls in the pursuit of a good time. He was champion of the local tennis club, a demon squash player, a keen golfer and captain of the local cricket team. He was a good swimmer, an expert dancer, a lot of fun—and the girls loved him. Very blond with dazzling blue eyes, a ready smile and a great deal of charm, it wasn't surprising that he was regarded as the local Casanova.

When she was being very honest with herself, Melissa admitted that she had wanted to work at St Biddulph's because it was only twenty miles away from the successful garden centre owned by Neville's parents. She had hoped she might see something of him but even in her wildest dreams, she hadn't expected him to give her so much of his time and attention. She might have been swept off her feet like so many other girls if there had been any hint of amorous intent in their relationship.

Neville had three sisters—and he seemed to look on her as a fourth, she thought wryly. But as he was a very good brother, generous and kind and attentive, she could only be grateful that he included her so often in his schemes for a good time.

Now he listened to the account of her interview with Matron and expressed an obviously genuine pleasure that she would be staying in the neighbourhood. She had told him that she would probably go back to London to work if her contract wasn't renewed.

'I'd have missed you,' he said carelessly, reaching for her hand and giving it a slight squeeze. 'Having you around has been rather nice, you know. You're such a sensible girl. I can *talk* to you. Most girls expect me to be making love to them all the time.'

'That must be a drawback,' she agreed demurely, eyes twinkling.

He grinned. 'A man likes to feel that he's wanted for more than his body, you know.'

Melissa chuckled. 'But it's such a beautiful body, Neville,' she teased, running her hand lightly over the muscles that rippled in his chest and shoulders.

He captured her hand. 'Behave yourself,' he reproached, blue eyes dancing. 'I thought *you* were different from other girls. I thought you *respected* me!'

'Idiot!' Laughing, she leaned over to kiss him lightly

on the cheek. He turned his head so that their lips met briefly. Melissa was startled. She drew away immediately. He had kissed her before, of course. Light, fraternal kisses that made no demands and offered no more than cousinly affection. They had never caused her heart to quicken or her pulses to beat a fraction faster. They knew each other too well. But there had been a hint of unexpected hunger in that touch of his mouth on her own, she thought.

He smiled at her, very warm. 'You're right,' he said softly. 'I *am* an idiot. It's taken me too long to stop thinking of you as little Melissa and to realise that you've grown into a very lovely woman . . .' He reached to cradle her face in both hands and kissed her again, too lightly to alarm her but with unmistakable promise.

'Oh, Neville . . . this is so sudden!' She was trying very hard to restore the light-hearted and comfortably familiar touch to their relationship. She smiled at him brightly, careful to keep any suspicion of coquetry from her eyes and voice.

'Well, we've wasted a lot of time,' he told her firmly. He put his arms about her, drew her close and kissed her.

This time, it wasn't at all cousinly or fraternal but very ardent. Melissa sensibly decided to lie back and enjoy the experience as he pressed her against the sofa cushions and kissed her expertly.

Being kissed by Neville was pleasant, if not as exciting as she had always imagined it would be. She decided that the fault lay in her lack of response rather than in his lovemaking. Anxious not to disappoint him, she took pains to pretend the kind of response that he probably found in other girls and kissed him back warmly.

There was a certain satisfaction in this unexpected embrace. Deep down, she had always been slightly envious of the many girls in his life. Like any woman, she had wondered why she was so unattractive or so undesirable in his eyes that he just didn't want to make love to her. It was reassuring to be treated as a woman at last. She had been the little cousin tagging along with good-looking Neville and his friends for too many years!

His lips strayed to her neck and then to the hollow of her throat. Melissa was not so naïve or inexperienced that she didn't realise the growing desire in the way that he held and kissed her. She wondered why she just didn't want him at all in the way that he so obviously wanted her.

His hand slid beneath the thin silk of her blouse to find the swell of her breast. Her flesh seemed to shrink from his touch. She told herself not to be such a prude and tried to relax in his unexpectedly sensual embrace.

He kissed and caressed her and murmured her name with longing and Melissa wondered if he really expected her to go along with his obvious intent. Perhaps other girls never refused him. But she was a virgin and she would need to be very much in love or overwhelmed by a tidal wave of longing to give herself to any man without hesitation.

Neville meant a lot to her and she trusted him but she knew that nothing would ever be the same between them if she allowed him to make love to her when there wasn't the least degree of loving on either side.

His body was heavy on her own and urgent with

passion. Meeting her instinctive resistance with patience, he kissed her, long and lingering, murmured soft endearments and reassurances and continued to coax her towards surrender. His persistent hand, twice pushed away, again found and curved about her small breast, his thumb sweeping across her nipple in confident caress. Melissa wondered in a very detached fashion why her body didn't stir as readily as it had for the merest brush of a stranger's arm . . .

The doorbell suddenly shrilled. She jumped. Neville tensed and then involuntarily relaxed his hold. Melissa gratefully seized the opportunity to wriggle out of his arms.

'Saved by the bell!' she declared lightly, brushing the fall of soft hair from her face and tucking her loosened blouse into the waistband of her skirt.

Neville smiled but there was annoyance and frustration in his blue eyes. 'Expecting someone?'

'Not really . . .'

'Then don't answer.' He caught her hand. 'Come back, love . . .' There was real urgency in his low tone.

The doorbell rang again. 'It might be important,' she demurred, hesitant.

'What could be more important than us?' he demanded softly.

She laughed and rumpled his blond hair in an affectionate caress. 'You're a terrible flirt!' she reproached.

He raised an eyebrow, looked hurt. 'What makes you think I'm flirting? I've never been more serious in my life!'

Melissa stared at him, startled and unsure. Then, not

knowing what to say or do in answer to that astonishing claim, she hurried to open the door to her caller.

The last person she expected to see was Ben Gregory, just about to turn away. She looked at him in surprise. She was suddenly conscious of her flushed face and tousled hair, and the undone button of her silk blouse that revealed the delicate curve of her breasts. The colour deepened in her face and she instinctively put a hand up to fasten that betraying button.

'I'm sorry to disturb you,' he said stonily.

'But you aren't!' It was oddly defensive.

Without thinking, she had thrust the door wide. She saw that the surgeon was looking beyond her at Neville who straightened up from the sofa cushions, thrusting his hands through his hair. Melissa felt uncomfortable, even a little guilty, although there was no flicker of expression in the grey eyes as Ben Gregory looked down at her once more.

It was impossible to know what he thought. But she was sure that she could give a fairly accurate guess . . .

CHAPTER THREE

MELISSA's chin went up slightly. As if she cared what Ben Gregory thought! 'What can I do for you?' she asked lightly.

He held out a slender gold bracelet. 'I think this must belong to you, Nurse Warren. I found it on the floor of the car. I decided to return it right away as it's obviously valuable and you might have been mourning its loss.'

She hadn't noticed that the fragile chain was missing from her wrist. There had been too many other things to think about since he had dropped her outside the house. The bracelet must have fallen off when she was struggling with the door handle, she realised.

She was delighted to have it back. It had great sentimental value for her, having been the last birthday gift from her parents before both were lost in a boating accident off the coast of Cornwall.

'Yes, it is mine!' she declared with a rush of relief. 'The catch is faulty and needs mending. I am grateful, Mr Gregory. It means such a lot to me!' She smiled at him warmly.

Being a modest girl, Melissa didn't realise that her smile was golden and effective when it leaped up so spontaneously. Nor did she know that it turned a merely pretty girl into a very lovely one, all in a moment. But if she had relied on the surgeon for enlightenment, she would have remained in ignorance. For he was in no mood that day to notice the charm of her smile or the sudden beauty of her small, fair face.

'Then I suggest that you have it repaired before you wear it again,' he said dryly, turning away.

Melissa felt snubbed by the dry words. She looked after him, not liking to close the door too soon. She felt that she shouldn't have kept him on the doorstep in such a rude fashion. It had been nice of him to return her bracelet so quickly. He was a busy man and he had problems and it had been unexpectedly thoughtful of him to bother about her anxiety. She wished that she *had* been anxious instead of so obviously unaware of its loss.

She watched him walk to the gate and his parked car. He didn't look back. He got into the car and drove away and Melissa closed the door, wondering why she wished she had invited him in and treated him like a friend instead of an unwelcome stranger. It might have lightened his obvious heaviness of heart just a little . . .

'Who was that?' Neville asked curiously.

'Ben Gregory. He's a surgeon. Senior Surgical Officer, actually,' she said absently, her mind still on that tall, departing and possibly disapproving figure. She felt that she hadn't really thanked him enough. She must remember to do so when they met again.

'Is he always so stiff-necked?' Neville drawled. 'Or was it because of me? Doesn't he approve of nurses fraternising with men outside the profession?'

Melissa gathered her wandering thoughts and smiled at him. He could be very perceptive and she didn't want him to suppose that there was anything going on between her and the surgeon. The very idea was not only impossible but quite ludicrous. 'We can't all marry doctors,' she said lightly. 'There aren't enough of them to go round!' She avoided the hand that was set to waylay her, scooping up her teacup and the empty lager can and heading for the kitchen.

Neville stood in the doorway and watched as she busied herself with quite unnecessary chores. 'Why are you suddenly fighting shy of me?' he asked.

'I'm not!' she said defensively. She laughed. 'That would be absurd when I've known you since I was in nappies!'

'It is absurd,' he agreed. He bent to bestow a fleeting kiss on her soft hair as she passed him on her way to a cupboard. 'Nothing's changed, love . . .'

She smiled at him quickly. 'Of course it hasn't!'

'Sorry . . . that was stupid! Things *have* changed, Melissa. The way I feel about you, for instance.'

He was too serious. Melissa looked at him doubtfully. 'Don't say any more . . . *please*!'

'I want you terribly,' he said quietly.

She shook her head. 'No, Neville.'

'Yes, Melissa.' He put his hands on her shoulders and turned her towards him. 'It's your own fault. You shouldn't have kissed me.'

'I've kissed you hundreds of times!'

'Perhaps it was never the right moment until today.' He drew her against him and held her. 'I've never thought of loving you, of making love to you. Suddenly I want to—more than anything in the world.' His arms tightened about her. His breath was warm, sighing through her soft hair.

'I like you better when you're fun,' Melissa said quietly, her face buried against his shoulder. She knew she was going to hurt him if he was serious—and he certainly seemed to be. She didn't want to hurt him. She cared about him too much.

'You've never seen any other side of me,' he told her confidently. 'I'll teach you to love me, darling.' He held her away slightly and smiled into her anxious eyes.

'I don't think loving is a lesson that can be learned, Neville. I think it either happens—or it doesn't!'

'Then I'll make it happen! Don't look so troubled. Don't you trust me? I promise I'll never do anything to hurt you or make you unhappy.'

'I know you wouldn't mean it even if you did,' she said slowly. 'You've broken an awful lot of hearts without ever meaning it, Neville.'

'Rubbish!' he declared briskly. 'I've had a lot of girls and maybe one or two of them have fallen in love with me but I've always let them down lightly. Most of them have married other men. Does that sound like undying love or broken hearts? Anyway, I've no intention of leaving *you* with a broken heart. You're much too important.'

He bent his head to kiss her. Melissa backed away. She saw a flicker of anger rather than dismay in the blue eyes. He was very used to getting what he wanted, she knew. She wondered if any girl had ever said no to him. She hoped he didn't suspect her of merely playing hard to get—that was the last thing in her mind.

'Don't kiss me again,' she said firmly. 'No, I mean it!' She put her hands against his chest to keep him at a safe distance and her eyes sparked with resolution. 'You must give me time to think, Neville. Heavens! Half an hour ago we were cousins and friends. Now you're trying to turn us into lovers all at once.'

He laughed. 'I believe in sweeping a girl off her feet. Giving her time to think can be fatal!'

'Well, you won't sweep *me* off my feet,' she told him firmly. 'You ought to know me better!' She shook her head at him in carefully light-hearted reproach. 'I certainly know you too well to rush into anything!'

He touched her cheek lightly, trailed his fingers down the slender lines of her neck to the provocative curve of her breast with a meaningful warmth in his blue eyes. 'Darling, don't you want me at all?' he said softly, very persuasive.

Melissa sighed. What *did* she say to that one? A blunt denial hovered on the tip of her tongue for she was an honest girl. But she felt that it would be too hurtful, too shattering to his pride. Yet it would probably be fatal to let him think that his kisses and caresses were potent enough to win him what he wanted in the end.

She didn't know why he left her quite so unmoved when he was so physically attractive and most girls probably fell into his arms with whoops of joy. It could only be a question of chemistry. For her, the vital ingredient seemed to be missing—that swift spark of desire! Or was it only that she had thought of him as a kind of brother for so long that it seemed almost sinful to imagine him as a lover in her arms?

It had occasionally crossed her mind to indulge in a romantic dream of loving her handsome cousin, of course. She wouldn't be human and a woman if it hadn't! But as it had always seemed so unlikely that he could ever love or want her, the pretty bubble of the dream had never been pricked by sharp reality. Until now.

She had left it too late to say anything at all. 'I see . . .' Neville's hand fell to his side. He smiled ruefully, shrugged. 'Can't win 'em all, I guess.'

Melissa couldn't bear the look in his eyes even if she did suspect that it was calculated to fill her with remorse. Impulsively, she put her arms about him. 'I can't promise that you won't lose in the end,' she warned. 'But if you really mean what you've been saying, I'm prepared to try it your way. But don't go too fast, Neville.' She smiled at him. 'Let me get used to the idea.'

He twined his fingers in the long, silky hair that framed her face and was so like his own in colour and texture. 'I have to get used to it, too. It's rather a shock to find that my feelings aren't at all cousinly after all these years.' He kissed her lightly. Suddenly, his eyes began to dance as he looked down at her, smiling. 'Be gentle with me, won't you?' he teased, mischievously.

The light words and the shared laughter eased a little disquiet in her heart, and Melissa stood more happily in his arms and allowed him to kiss her. But she was ready to stiffen and draw away if that kiss became too ardent and too demanding. He seemed to sense her mood for he released her almost immediately.

'I came to take you out,' he told her carelessly. 'We seem to have been side-tracked! In the nicest possible way, of course.' He smiled. 'I knew you were off duty and I brought a picnic with me. It's quite hot enough for the beach, don't you think? I've some champagne packed in ice in the boot but it's probably melted by this time.'

'Champagne!' Melissa laughed at him. 'You really are the most extravagant man I know!'

'Well, it's useful for any occasion. I didn't know if you'd want to celebrate after your interview or if you'd want cheering up—and champagne is ideal for either purpose.'

He was so *nice*, she thought warmly. How many men would have bothered to remember that this was the day of her interview with Matron let alone take pains to be on hand to congratulate her or to commiserate with her on the result? No wonder other women found it so easy to love him. No wonder he was really very dear to her even if she couldn't convince herself that her feeling for him would ever turn into loving . . .

Baymouth was a popular holiday resort with its impressive esplanade, two piers and a modern leisure complex, its amusement arcades and non-stop holiday entertainment and bustling shops. The coastline provided golden miles of sand and low, rambling cliffs that were a delight to explore, and there were lots of lovely spots for sunbathing or family picnics or lovers in search of privacy.

Neville drove to a favourite place some distance from the town. Here, there was a break in the cliffs and a small village bordered on an expanse of sand dunes and marram grass before a wide stretch of sun-soaked beach. There was a cluster of small holiday bungalows actually on the beach among the dunes but it was so early in the season that there were few people about.

They swam and sunbathed and enjoyed their picnic and the warm champagne. Melissa was relieved that he was his usual easy-going and cheerful self. Those moments of ardent lovemaking might never have happened. It seemed that he had taken her words to heart and meant to give her plenty of time to adjust to the sudden change in their relationship.

She wasn't sure that she would ever get used to it, she thought wryly, lying beside him in the sun, very conscious of his lean body stretched at her side, their hands almost touching. Youthful admiration for her Greek god of a cousin was one thing. She couldn't help feeling that looking upon him as a lover was a very different matter.

He was very lithe, very tanned, very handsome with his silvery blond hair and almost too-perfect features and the charm of his ready smile. She really ought to want him. Melissa might have wondered if she was frigid if her body's response to a very different man wasn't still so vividly in her mind for all her efforts to forget it. Ben Gregory had made an unconscious and very potent impact on her senses, it seemed—without even trying!

For he wasn't at all interested in her as a woman, she felt. She wondered if it was true that he had a girl in Bury St Edmunds. He certainly seemed to have no time at all for any of the nurses who had been casting out lures for the surgeon since his arrival at St Biddulph's.

His arm had brushed her quite by accident. He hadn't even noticed—he certainly hadn't realised her instinctive and rather dismaying reaction to his physical magnetism.

He had the kind of looks that most women would find fascinating and exciting, and he was really too attractive for his own good—or anyone else's, she thought dryly. It seemed a cruel trick of nature that he should be a cold and unfeeling man for all that hint of sensuality that had triggered her to a sudden and unwelcome wanting.

Surgery was his first love, she felt—even a passion with him. His fiancée probably came a very poor second to his dedication and ambition—if she existed at all! It wasn't unknown for a man to invent such a good excuse for ignoring invitations from the women who were eager to open their arms to him. Somehow, she just couldn't imagine Ben Gregory in the throes of ardent desire for any woman and he certainly didn't seem to be the marrying kind. She didn't think that any woman would want to marry him either—unless she was prepared to be frozen to death.

Neville wasn't the marrying kind either, she mused soberly, studying him as he drowsed in the hot sun. She was rather troubled by his careless talk of loving that wasn't likely to lead to an offer of marriage. He seemed so confident that he could persuade her to love him—and then what?

Melissa enjoyed nursing but, like any other girl, she had dreams of husband, home and family at some time in the future. She just didn't believe it would happen if she became involved with Neville. He would never give up the freedom that was so precious to him for any woman's sake, she was sure. She would be wise to hang on to her heart with both hands rather than lose it to him for all his niceness and charm, and the love of life that made him such fun to be with.

Neville really didn't take anything very seriously— while Ben Gregory seemed to take everything much too seriously. Her ideal man was probably a blend of the two, she thought lightly. Perhaps she ought to wait for him to come along before falling headlong into love. But ideal men were few and far between, she suspected . . .

Some time later, scrambling over the dunes on the way back to the car, she was surprised to recognise the tall figure of the surgeon standing at the door of one of the wooden bungalows. The sliding sun caught the bronze of his hair and turned it to bright copper, it fell full across the lean, attractive face with the deep-set eyes and mobile mouth. He had changed from the formal grey suit into jeans and a thin sweatshirt, he didn't seem quite so aloof as usual.

'Hallo!' Melissa exclaimed, pausing, slightly out of breath after hurrying to catch up with Neville who had gone on with the picnic basket, rugs and radio. 'Is that where you live?' she asked impulsively, unable to keep the astonished curiosity out of her tone.

'Temporarily,' he said, rather curtly. 'It belongs to a friend and I've borrowed it while I look around for a house in the area.'

'I envy you,' she said lightly. 'I'd love to live right on the beach.'

'You're very young.' He made it sound like an offence. 'I can do without sand in my food and the wind whistling around the dunes all night. But I daresay it would seem an adventure to you.'

Melissa felt rather crushed. 'It's certainly different.' She turned to walk on, sensing that Neville was watching from the parked car. She was suddenly conscious of the brevity of her white shorts and sun-top, although he didn't seem to be at all aware of her slender, sun-kissed body and the shapely length of her legs. She hesitated, turned. 'When you came with my bracelet . . .' She broke off, absurdly embarrassed but anxious that he shouldn't think ill of her, without quite knowing why. 'It wasn't what you thought, you know,' she said proudly. It sounded so lame to her own ears that she immediately wished she hadn't said anything at all. She didn't have to explain anything away to Ben Gregory. She didn't even like him!

He raised an eyebrow. 'I don't know that I thought anything. Your personal life is not my concern.'

'No,' she agreed, her face flaming. 'But I wouldn't want you to have the wrong impression.'

'Does it matter?' He was very cool.

'It does to me!' It was quick, slightly tart.

He shrugged. 'I'm sure that you're a very nice girl,' he said carelessly, with great indifference. 'And I didn't leap to the wrong conclusion. Only the right one.'

She wasn't sure that she liked the cryptic flavour of the words. But before she could demand an explanation, Neville called, sounding impatient, and she hurried towards the car.

The surgeon moved from the bungalow with long strides to pick up the thin-strapped sandal that had slipped from the bundle of clothes and towels beneath her arm. 'Nurse Warren!'

Melissa turned. Then she hurried back to him at the sight of the shoe he held out to her. 'Thank you . . .'

'You make a habit of mislaying things. Thank God you aren't a surgeon,' he said dryly.

She looked at him quickly, suspecting that sardonic note in his deep voice. There wasn't even the trace of a twinkle in the grey eyes. She decided to smile, just the same. It wasn't the warm and spontaneous smile that she bestowed on her friends, but it held a little of its usual magic. Ben Gregory looked down at her with a faint frown in his eyes. Then he turned abruptly and walked back to the beach bungalow without another word.

Feeling snubbed, Melissa ran the last few yards to join Neville. He looked curiously at her flushed face and suspiciously bright eyes. 'That's the same fellow,' he said.

She nodded. 'Sarcastic devil,' she said, with feeling.

He stiffened. 'Why? What did he say?' He looked towards the bungalow. But there was no sign of the man who had been standing in the doorway. 'Shall I sort him out?' he demanded, ready to defend her from insult.

Melissa shook her head. 'No. He didn't really say much. I'm just over-sensitive. I don't particularly like him, Neville, so I expect I'm too quick to resent his attitude.'

'Fancies you, does he?' Neville reversed the car with care, looking over his shoulder, but narrowly missed a white Mercedes with a personalised number plate.

Melissa glanced at the familiar car. It hadn't been parked in that particular spot when they arrived at the beach. 'Far from it! If he wasn't engaged to some girl, I'd declare that he hates all women!'

She didn't want to talk about Ben Gregory and she carefully changed the subject as the sleek sports car zoomed away from the cluster of bungalows and the few cottages surrounding the pub that made up the village.

Neville took her to the flat so that she could dress for the evening. He sat down to watch the flickering screen of the ancient television set while she showered the sand from her body and put on a pretty floral frock and brushed her hair until it shone, curling slightly on her shoulders.

Melissa looked at herself in the mirror and thought of Neville's careless words. *'Fancies you, does he?'* She thought dryly that Ben Gregory hadn't even known the colour of her hair after three weeks of working with her, and that proved just how much interest he had taken in his theatre nurse.

On the beach, his glance had swept quite indifferently over her near-nude body with its youthful curves that attracted admiration from other men. She might have been lying on an operating table for all the reaction in those grey eyes! With a slightly rueful smile, she admitted that he would have taken much more interest in her body in those circumstances.

So, he was looking for a house in Baymouth. That implied that he meant to settle in the area, perhaps he had plans to be married in the near future. Maybe the nurse from Bury St Edmunds would come to work at St Biddulph's once she was married to the surgeon. It would be interesting to discover if he became more human once he was married.

At the moment, he didn't seem to be enjoying his bachelor existence in that shanty by the sea. It was very little more, Melissa thought bluntly. Those ramshackle bungalows weren't meant to be lived in for any length of time and they had few of the modern conveniences that a man like Ben Gregory would miss. At this time of year the place was almost deserted when the sun went down, for few people lived in that tiny village all the year round. It must be lonely and rather bleak when the sun didn't shine. Not the best of places for a man with things on his mind.

Melissa suddenly remembered the way he had looked in the pub garden at lunch-time—so tense and unhappy, burdened by his thoughts. She felt she could have been nicer to him, smiled with rather more warmth, treated him with rather more friendliness. Even though he had snubbed her and chilled her with his manner and his cold words, his obvious impatience and lack of interest. Perhaps he had very good reason for that grim, off-putting mood. She couldn't help wondering at the nature of the news which had depressed him so much.

She wondered why she was still thinking about Ben Gregory, dawdling in her bedroom while Neville waited to take her out for a meal and a show. Considering she didn't really like the surgeon he seemed to be taking up an awful lot of her attention, she scolded herself—and thrust him from her mind as Neville appeared in the doorway to hurry her up . . .

CHAPTER FOUR

MELISSA untied the strings of her mask and drew it from her face with a sigh of relief. She was hot and tired from the long spell of assisting beneath the arc lights, the need to be constantly on her toes to please a demanding surgeon, and the knowledge that she had been too late to bed on the previous night.

It had been a heavy list that day without the car crash almost outside the hospital gates that had made further demands on the duty surgical team. One casualty had died on the operating table, too badly injured to save when he reached Theatres, although Ben Gregory had fought against all odds for his life.

Watching, Melissa had seen the sweat breaking out on his brow and moved to wipe it away with a sterile towel before it trickled into his eyes. She had observed his intense and single-minded concentration as he worked against time and the anaesthetist's quiet warning that the patient was failing fast.

She had handed the prepared hypodermic to him before he could demand it and watched as he plunged the needle deep into the heart muscles of his patient. He had laboured to force that heart to beat again, refusing to admit defeat, for nearly half an hour. Then, for the first time, she had heard him swear with savage fury at his failure, not quite beneath his breath. Like every surgeon, he hated to lose a patient—and he felt it even more deeply when it was a child, robbed of life when it was scarcely begun.

But they had managed to save three of the lives that had been so nearly lost through careless driving on a wet road. The weather had suddenly broken that morning with a succession of heavy storms. In Theatres they had been much too busy throughout a long and weary day to know that the sun was no longer shining over Baymouth.

Melissa wasn't just tired. She felt as though every nerve in her body was at full stretch. Ben Gregory's tension and anger seemed to have communicated itself to her all day. His mood had been just as grim as it had been on the previous day when he arrived in Theatres to begin the day's list, and he looked as if he hadn't slept at all. She had received only the curtest of nods in answer to a greeting that she had tried to infuse with some friendliness. Endeavouring to thank him again properly for finding and returning her bracelet and trying to explain something of what it meant to her, he had cut her short and walked away to scrub up.

In return for the snub, Melissa had been just as efficient and hard-working as she knew how to be, never unbending for a single moment within sight or sound of the surgeon, determined to be just the kind of robot nurse that he obviously preferred to have around him while he worked. She had striven to be just as aloof and impersonal and inhuman as he was—and that had been a strain for a naturally warm-hearted and friendly girl.

She hadn't been the only one to suffer at his hands that day. The merciless tongue with its savage irony had lashed everyone during the day. He had reduced one nurse to tears, alienated the porters, and even managed to ruffle Theatre Sister who was the sweetest and most equable of women.

He had been at odds with himself and the world, Melissa thought. He had seemed bent on destroying the warm and friendly atmosphere of Theatres, built up over months of cheerful camaraderie and tolerance by the rest of the staff. For the best part of the day he had worked in near-silence, broken only by his terse instructions, seemingly untroubled by or serenely unconscious of the enmity and resentment that he was arousing on all sides. He had a job to do and he was doing it to the best of his ability and he expected everyone else to be as unaffected by the atmosphere as himself—or so his attitude implied.

She looked at him now through the glass window of the ante-room as he divested himself of mask and gown and pulled the green cap from his head. His hair was rumpled, darkened by damp and inclined to curl, she noticed. He looked white and drawn with weariness, and the skin seemed stretched tight by tension across his cheekbones. She saw the tensing of his jaw muscles and wondered if the darkening of his grey eyes was a trick of the light or caused by the throbbing of a headache.

Something had to be very wrong, Melissa thought, with the instinctive concern that made her such a good and caring nurse. He had been impersonal, and demanding and difficult during those first weeks at St Biddulph's, but he hadn't been savagely bent on making everyone's life a misery. Perhaps it was just a foolish fancy but she couldn't help feeling that he was lashing out like a wounded animal—rejecting even the least hint of sympathy or concern rather than admit to his hurt.

He glanced at her as though he suddenly sensed her gaze and she saw him frown. Then he turned his back to her and bent over the basin to sluice cold water over his face and hair.

Melissa knew she should leave the theatre and allow the staff to begin the task of tidying up. But she found it impossible to walk out on him without a word as everyone else in the team had done. Maybe it wasn't wanted, maybe it wasn't even justified, but she felt desperately sorry for him.

Automatically she reached for a towel and went to hand it to him as he surfaced, gasping. He buried his face in the towel, rubbed at his wet hair. Melissa wished she'd thrown it at him as a surge of annoyance replaced that absurd compassion. Not a word of thanks! She might as well *be* the robot she had tried all day to be just to please him, she thought bitterly.

'It's been a bloody day,' he said as he lowered the towel and tossed it into the 'dirty' bin on top of his gown.

'Yes, it has,' she said bluntly, with feeling. 'And you've been the bloodiest part of it!' Perhaps she shouldn't talk so to the Senior Surgical Officer who had the power to report her to Matron and even have her dismissed, but she had been bottling up her feelings all day and the cool indifference of that comment had been the last straw.

'That's true,' he agreed.

Melissa's eyes widened. 'I think you must be a very unhappy man,' she heard herself saying, much to her own surprise.

He looked down at her for a long moment and she felt the colour surging into her face. But she saw that he didn't resent her words. He seemed to be considering her as a person for the first time.

'Bad, my dear. Not sad,' he corrected smoothly with the faintest of smiles in his eyes. 'No man likes to be made to look a fool and that's just happened to me. But I ought not to vent my rage on everyone in sight. I daresay I'm the most unpopular man in the place right now?'

'Well, you haven't any friends!' she told him with truth.

The surgeon shrugged. 'Then I must drown my sorrows alone—and there's no sadder sight than a lonely drunk. I mean to get very, very drunk tonight, Nurse Warren. I don't suppose you'd care to join me?'

'No,' she said, startled.

'Then you aren't my friend, either, it seems. Now, that *does* hurt.'

Melissa looked at him doubtfully, deciding that he was the most enigmatic man. It was impossible to know if he meant anything he said. She had never realised just how much a smile could convey—and he didn't smile at all. Not even when he was joking—and surely that had been a joke?

'You shouldn't talk so wildly, Mr Gregory,' she rebuked him, just as though he was a recalcitrant patient. 'I think you ought to go home and get some sleep and forget about getting drunk. You look exhausted.'

'I am exhausted. Anger is a very exhausting emotion—and I've never been so angry in my life as I am at present.' A nerve throbbed in his cheek as he spoke. He leaned against the door frame and spread his powerful hands, and looked at them with suddenly blazing eyes. 'I'm a surgeon, dedicated to saving life with these hands.

Right now I feel like using them to *take* life—and you tell me to go home and sleep. God, I wish I could!'

Melissa was shocked by the naked passion in his eyes and voice. She hadn't thought him capable of it. She had thought him cold and unfeeling while he was struggling through the days with murder in his heart.

'Is it something to do with your fiancée . . . ?' Guided only by instinct, she asked the question very gently, wondering how she dared to approach such an un-approachable man. But surely only the loss of something or someone he loved very much could inspire so much hurt and suffering, transmuted into anger in sheer self-defence.

'My ex-fiancée.' It was very cold, very cutting. 'I've wasted four years of my life on a woman who is about to marry my best friend. *My best friend!* What a misnomer!' The words seemed to be forced from him by the need to tell someone—anyone.

'I'm sorry,' Melissa said quietly.

'For *me*?' He stiffened. 'Don't be sorry for me, Nurse Warren! The mess isn't of my making and *I* won't have any regrets! Save your sympathy for fools like those two who'll make each other mad or miserable in six months!'

She understood the fierce pride that rejected pity. She thought that he must have loved the girl very much—and trusted his friend. She ached with compassion for him. Being a practical girl, she said levelly, 'I expect you'd like some tea, Mr Gregory. I know I would. It's been a long day.'

He put a hand briefly on her shoulder, squeezed. 'Tea and sympathy. Just what I'd expect from a good nurse.' A faint flush of pleased surprise swept into her face as he looked down at her. His hand fell away abruptly. 'No, I don't want tea, Nurse Warren.' He walked away from her towards the surgeons' changing-room. 'I believe your car is still out of action,' he said carelessly, over his shoulder. 'I'll give you a lift if you can be ready in ten minutes.'

He didn't wait for a reply.

Melissa looked at the firmly closed door and wondered why her body was tingling as if that strong hand still rested on her shoulder.

Then she hurried away to change from her surgical greens to be ready in time. He wasn't the kind of man to keep waiting. She suspected that he simply wouldn't wait.

The surgeon drove the few miles in silence as though he regretted having told her so much of his affairs. Melissa was too tired to talk. Tired and rather troubled to realise the extent of her concern for him. How could she care so deeply for his hurt and his disappointment when she really didn't like him very much? Why couldn't she shrug and dismiss him and turn her thoughts to Neville and his sudden and surprising need of her?

Ben Gregory didn't need her liking or her sympathy and there was nothing she could do to see him through this bad patch in his life, she told herself firmly. She really didn't want to be involved in any way with him.

They reached the house and he halted the car outside the shabby, unpainted gates and switched off the engine. 'May I come in?' he asked abruptly. 'I want to talk to you.'

Melissa was startled and rather dismayed by the unexpected words. 'Yes . . . yes, of course,' she said uncertainly.

He followed her along the narrow, overgrown path to the side of the house and she found her key in her uniform pocket and opened the door. She stooped to scoop up the letters that had arrived after she'd left for the hospital that morning. She put them on the table then smiled at him and tried to sound hospitable as she said, 'Do sit down, Mr Gregory.' She hoped he didn't mean to stay for more than a few minutes. She wanted to relax and unwind after the hectic day and he was making her as tense as himself, she thought wryly.

'Thank you.' He lowered himself into a chair and looked about him with interest. The evening was overcast. The room seemed gloomy despite the cheerful curtains and cushions and the colourful prints on the walls. 'This is very homely.'

'No, it isn't. It's a dreadful place,' Melissa said brightly. 'But it's all I can afford for the time being. I'd much rather live in your bungalow on the beach.'

'You're welcome to it,' he told her shortly. 'It's the most desolate spot on earth just now.' He leaned back in his chair like a very tired man. 'I should like that tea, after all. If you don't mind?'

Melissa was in two minds about it, but she assured him that it was no trouble. She went into the kitchen, filled the kettle and took down cups, busying herself with the mundane routine of tea-making to keep her mind from worrying at his presence in the other room and his surprising wish to talk to her. She couldn't think what he had to say to her. She didn't really want him in the flat.

It was too absurd to feel that she didn't trust him when

he was so aloof, so indifferent. She just didn't like that foolish and persistent throb of excitement that he invoked too easily. With a look, with a touch, just by being in the same, small room as herself. And she was terrified that he might sense it. There was nothing worse than wanting a man who obviously wasn't aware of her as a woman, she thought ruefully.

She didn't like to leave him alone too long. She went back into the sitting-room and found him relaxed, eyes closed, long legs outstretched and hands thrust deep into his trouser pockets. He didn't move. She said his name quietly. The heavy eyelids didn't even flicker. A wave of his thick auburn hair fell across his brow.

Melissa looked at the sleeping surgeon and felt an odd tremor near her heart. He looked terribly vulnerable, and for some ridiculous reason she longed to put her arms about him and hold him and soothe away the anger and the bitterness and the hate.

She made the tea and took it in on a tray. He still didn't stir. She sat down on the sofa and drank her own tea and studied him while he slept, wondering why she had never particularly liked him even when he wasn't treating her like dirt. It must have been a defensive kind of dislike, she decided. She had probably been trying to protect herself from liking him too much. Being a very honest girl with the courage to face facts, she admitted that it hadn't worked.

This difficult, demanding man tugged at her heart-strings and stirred her senses and put a lot of foolish romantic notions into her normally sensible head without even trying, she thought wryly. It seemed that Neville had left it just too late to realise that he could love the little cousin who had hero-worshipped him for years. She knew now with a sudden blinding clarity that she could never love him at all.

She was a long way from loving Ben Gregory, too. But he had that indefinable quality that Neville lacked for her. It wasn't just the very potent sexuality that found its echo in her own unawakened body. She knew instinctively that they had a great deal to give each other.

Her heart quickened at the thought of inspiring him to only a little of the passion that he obviously felt for the woman who had let him down so badly—and then it sank at the absurdity of the hope that she might ever mean very much to the proud and clever surgeon. He could take his pick from a dozen women if he wished, all more attractive than herself!

'I'm not asleep, you know,' he said quietly, making her jump.

'Then you're cheating!' she exclaimed, very light.

'I'm listening to your busy thoughts. Scurry, scurry, whisper, whisper. Like a lot of startled mice.' He opened his eyes to look at her with a slightly sardonic gleam in the grey depths.

Melissa hoped he didn't know what had been hurtling through her mind while she waited patiently for him to wake. 'I'm afraid your tea is cold.'

'Yes, I'm sorry. It just seemed too much effort to move.' He rose abruptly from the chair, towering above her in the small room. 'But I'm afraid I'm encroaching on your evening . . .'

'I'm not doing anything with it. You don't have to rush away.' She hadn't meant it to sound like blatant encouragement, it had just come out that way, she realised, dismayed.

The surgeon watched the slow tide of colour staining her fair skin and then he said lightly, 'You refused to get drunk with me. Will you come for a meal, instead? We both need to eat, after all.'

It was too casually said to be flattering. Melissa didn't think he could really want to sit in a restaurant and play host when he was so weary. She knew he would only make the effort if she accepted the unexpected invitation.

'I think I'm rather too tired to change and go out, quite honestly,' she said carefully. 'But I could cook something if you'd like to stay?'

His eyes narrowed abruptly. 'Still feeling sorry for me, Nurse Warren?'

She wondered if any woman could overcome that fierce and sensitive pride now that he had been so badly hurt. 'No, I'm not,' she returned. 'You're feeling sorry enough for two, I think.' Her smile took the sting from the blunt words. 'Do stay. As you say, we both need to eat, and I've some steaks and salad in the fridge.' She picked up the tea tray. 'Besides, you still haven't told me what you wanted to talk to me about.'

'Oh, that was an excuse. I didn't feel like driving any further,' he said coolly.

Melissa carried the tray into the kitchen and wondered if it would have killed him to admit that he had needed her company—if only because he couldn't bear the thought of being on his own that evening. She decided that he would probably have choked on his pride.

He followed her. In that tiny room, she was much too conscious of him for comfort, she discovered.

'Can I help?'

He was behind her as she turned from the fridge. Finding her head on a level with his chin, feeling absurdly overwhelmed by his height and the hint of masculine strength in his unexpected nearness, she thought it best not to look up into those penetrating grey eyes. 'You could go and sit down,' she said firmly. 'Play some records or watch television or read a paper. Relax and make yourself at home while I cook the steaks.'

He put his hand beneath her chin and tilted her face. He was almost impatient. 'Don't talk to my tie, Melissa. I'm up here.'

Her heart shook at the sound of her name on his lips for the first time. 'You're in the way,' she said lightly, hoping to hide the quiver of her senses at his touch and the rather disturbing look in his eyes.

He kissed her, taking her lips as though they belonged to him with a kind of hunger that rocked her from head to toe with sudden delight. She was so startled that it didn't occur to her to protest, to back away. She was much too busy fighting that flood of delicious wanting.

He put an arm about her and drew her to him roughly and she felt the powerful, exciting throb of his body. His kiss became deeper, more sensual, fiercely demanding and Melissa slid her arms up and around his neck and kissed him back on a surging tide of desire that discounted everything else.

He was making very potent love to her with his lips, his hands, his body against her own, and she was suddenly plunged into very deep waters and didn't seem to care if she drowned in them as long as his arms were about her.

'Come to bed,' he said against her mouth, urgent.

'What about the steaks . . .?' It was a very weak protest.

'Later. I want you *now*.'

He was too forceful to be denied. And Melissa was too weak with wanting, melting before the fire and the passion of his embrace. She found herself swept up into strong arms and carried into the bedroom. He kissed her as he laid her down on the bed and the leaping, insistent flame of her response was all the encouragement he needed.

She had never felt this way before. She had never understood the power and the glory and the magnificence of this kind of loving. She had never wanted any man so much that nothing in the world mattered but his arms about her and his mouth on her own, his body urging her towards the towering peaks of ecstasy.

Until now . . .

He wasn't gentle. He wasn't inclined to be patient. He was eager, trembling with the force of his passion, taking her swiftly and so tumultuously that pain and pleasure mingled in such delight that she couldn't mourn the virginity that was lost for ever on that tidal wave of mutual wanting. She doubted if he even knew that he was the first man to sweep her to that glorious fulfilment with the powerful thrust of his own need.

Their bodies still entwined, hearts thudding in unison, he lay with his lips buried in the hollow of her throat and a hand still cupping her breast, shuddering slightly from the effects of that sensual and stirring encounter.

Melissa ran her hand over his bare back with its rippling muscles and then stroked the bronze hair that was inclined to curl about her fingers, marvelling that near-strangers could create that kind of heaven for each other.

Ben stirred and raised his head to look at her. He wasn't smiling but there was a warmth in his eyes that she had never seen before and her heart suddenly swelled with an emotion even greater than the desire that had stormed so suddenly into her life and changed it irrevocably. She touched her hand to his lean cheek with tenderness. The gesture said all that she couldn't find words or voice to say in that moment.

Abruptly, he gathered her close and kissed her and his lips lingered on a sigh of content. She knew that all his tension had ebbed away with their lovemaking and she didn't have the least regret that she had given herself without hesitation.

'I needed you,' he said quietly.

She nodded. 'I know.'

Suddenly, he smiled. There was quite breathtaking enchantment in that rare smile that curved the mobile mouth and enriched his good looks, chasing the grim shadows from his grey eyes. 'I hope you like me a little better now, Nurse Warren,' he teased gently.

Absurdly, Melissa wanted to cry.

She choked back the tears and said lightly, 'Just a little. I think you might grow on me with time, Mr Gregory.'

Somehow it was too soon to tell him that she loved him as much now as she ever would . . . with all her heart and for ever.

CHAPTER FIVE

BEN showered while she cooked the steaks and laid the table. He came into the kitchen to find her and dropped a light kiss on the back of her neck.

Melissa smiled over her shoulder at him. 'Almost ready . . .'

'You really are the most efficient girl,' he approved, observing the ready-tossed salad, the bottle of wine and the other preparations for the meal. 'What a marvellous wife you'll make for some man one day!'

The careless words struck a savage blow at a foolish hope that she hadn't admitted to herself until that moment. But had she really imagined that someone like Ben might marry her eventually? Had she really supposed that his urgent lovemaking might be born of more than a fleeting sexual need?

He wouldn't have an ounce of patience with that kind of romantic nonsense, she felt. 'I must take care to marry a man who'll appreciate me,' she returned brightly.

'He'll be a fool if he doesn't.' His tone softened the curt words. He turned her to him and slid his strong hands beneath the silk of her robe to caress her body with a lover's confidence. He looked down at her with a glow in his eyes that quickened her anew. 'You're enchanting,' he said softly. 'Exciting. I want you all over again . . .'

Melissa drew away. 'This time we have the steaks,' she said firmly.

Ben threw back his head and laughed, delighting her. He was too serious, too intense. She felt that he had probably never laughed enough in his life. He needed to laugh more, to relax and enjoy life. Humour could be healing, too.

The steaks were rescued just in time and they sat down to eat and washed down the simple meal with a rather good wine that had been a present from Neville. She had been saving it for an occasion—this seemed to be just the occasion worthy of it, she thought, a little dryly. Like a girl's confirmation and coming-of-age, that first step across the dividing line between virginity and full womanhood was surely a milestone in her life.

Over the meal, she learned a little more about the man she loved. That he had qualified at the Central where his father had once been a surgeon, well-known and highly respected. That, like herself, he had lost both his parents. He had a brother while Melissa was an only child. He was thirty-one to her twenty-three.

She told him a little about herself, too. Her days at Hartlake, the impulse and the family link that had brought her to Baymouth and St Biddulph's, how much she had enjoyed the last six months. This didn't draw him to tell her why he had come to work in the new hospital on the Norfolk coast, and he carefully didn't mention his previous job or the link with Bury St Edmunds. She didn't want to remind him. She was only too thankful to have driven that terrible bleakness from his handsome face, if only temporarily.

She was beginning to watch for the little smile in his

eyes that seemed much dearer than the ready smiles that lit up the whole of other men's faces. She was beginning to appreciate the sardonic sense of humour and the deceptively straight-faced utterances. She was beginning to love him too much for peace of mind, she thought wryly, curling up on the sofa with feet tucked beneath her while Ben made coffee.

Melissa hugged her arms across breasts that were tender from being crushed against him and knew that her whole body was still vibrant and glowing from that magical, almost mystical experience. She was glad that she had realised she was falling in love with him before he swept her into bed or she might have had to wonder if the warmth about her heart was only the after-glow of that lovemaking.

She didn't think she would have the heart to send him off to that lonely bungalow on a deserted beach if he wished to stay. She longed to lie in his arms and know the warm reassurances of his presence through the night. She felt as if she never wanted him to leave her again.

But that was something that she must carefully keep to herself, she realised. For no man liked too much intensity of emotion at the beginning of a new relationship and nothing scared him off quicker than the slightest hint of possessiveness in a woman's attitude, she thought wryly.

Coming in behind her, he ran a hand over the smooth fall of her blonde hair and she smiled up at him swiftly. His hand lingered briefly at her shoulder. He bent to kiss her lightly and she said his name with a surge of tenderness.

'That's my answer,' he said quietly and she looked at

him with a question in her dark blue eyes. 'I wasn't sure if I should go or stay.'

She reached impulsively for his hand and took it to her breast in a gesture that implied her readiness to give for his delight and her own. 'Stay. I want you all over again . . .' She echoed his own words with a slight catch of her breath.

Later, he made slow and very sensuous love to her with the expertise of experience and Melissa found that he could be gentle and patient and very tender, and that there was more than one kind of heaven to be found in a man's embrace. She knew that his lovemaking had spoiled her for any other man. As long as she lived, she would only want Ben's arms about her, his kisses, his caresses, his skilled and sensitive and splendid loving.

With a full heart, she lay with her arm across him while he slept and the tears rolled gently down her cheeks. Loving him, she longed to tell him so. But silence was forced on her by the knowledge that he loved the woman who had let him down. Only hurt and disappointment and pride had driven him into her arms. These few hours probably meant little to him. They meant all the world to her and would never be forgotten. Ben was a memory to keep and cherish all her life. He was a man to love all her life. She couldn't believe it possible that he would ever love her. And although strangers had become lovers all in a moment, it didn't necessarily mean that they were friends . . .

In the morning, Melissa woke to find that she was alone in the flat. She had a vague memory of stirring at first light to the coolness of his lips on her own and then slipping back into sleep.

She touched the hollow in the pillow where his handsome head had rested. She thought how right and natural it had seemed to lie with him through the night, his body curving about her own as though they had belonged together since the beginning of time. She had gone to sleep with his arms about her and she had wanted to wake with them still encircling her, and she felt cheated and lost without him. Perhaps he had suffered a sudden revulsion of feeling and decided that he couldn't face the intimacy of breakfast with a virtual stranger.

She still marvelled that they had become lovers so suddenly. She hadn't thought that she even liked him and he had seemed indifferent to her. But they had been caught up in a vortex of powerful and primitive emotion with the inevitable result.

She had been a virgin. Ben hadn't seemed to realise or care. Now an unforgettable bond had been created between them, Melissa felt. For if she never saw him again in her life, a woman never forgot her initiation into the world of sexual delight or the man who was responsible for it.

For her, passion had been so touched with love that she didn't know where one began and the other ended. For him, it had probably been no more than a fleeting sexual encounter like many others in a sensual man's life, unimportant and easily forgotten.

As she prepared for the day's work, the small flat seemed filled with his presence. *There* he had relaxed in the wing-backed chair and yielded to his utter weariness. *There* he had kissed her on that soaring tide of desire. *There* they had eaten and talked and got to know each other a little better. *There* she had basked in the enchantment of his smile for the first time and fallen under its spell for ever.

She was consumed with the longing to see him, to talk to him, and she was thankful that he was operating again that day. Hopefully, it would be a short list and not too demanding, he would be able to hand over some of the cases to the duty surgeon.

It happened to be Jamie Greaves that day and the two surgeons came into Theatres together, talking. Melissa kept her head bent over the laid-up trolley, checking the array of gleaming instruments and the prepared hypodermics, and mentally reviewing the procedure for the ganglionectomy that was first on the list. Her heart was thumping so hard against her ribs that she was sure that it could be heard.

'Good morning, Nurse Warren.'

It was so cool, so formal, that it steadied her tumultuous heart. She glanced up, the efficient theatre nurse interrupted in a routine task, and said briskly, 'Good morning, Mr Gregory . . . Mr Greaves. First patient's on the way to Theatres and we're quite ready for you . . .'

The grey eyes met her own as if she was a stranger. Disappointed, slightly chilled, Melissa asked herself what she had expected. He was a professional, a dedicated surgeon, a man who lived for his work. Before, anger had been so fierce in him that it had almost broken through the natural reserve of a very proud man. It had certainly coloured his attitude to those around him even if his work hadn't actually suffered. But ordinary sentiment, a hangover from lovemaking that had transformed her life but was probably just a casual experience for him, wasn't likely to interfere with the day's list and the waiting patients.

Melissa knew she must take her cue from him. So she looked back at him as if those magic moments had never happened and then turned away to continue counting swabs with a very necessary concentration.

The two surgeons worked steadily through the list. The ganglionectomy, a straightforward tonsillectomy, two hernia repairs and a gall bladder removal. When the last patient was trundled out of the theatre into the recovery room Ben nodded curtly to the anaesthetist and Jamie and strode away to change.

'Thank God his temper was a bit sweeter today,' Jamie said quietly.

The anaesthetist was fiddling with taps and levers and didn't answer. Melissa pulled down her green mask and smiled at the surgeon. Everyone liked Jamie.

'He's probably had things on his mind,' she said lightly.

'He should have my mortgage and the bills and a teething baby and a wife who keeps threatening to run home to mother,' Jamie retorted with feeling.

Melissa looked at him quickly. He was always so cheerful and even-tempered and happy-go-lucky that it was easy to forget that he had problems, like so many young doctors who had married too soon and worked very long hours and struggled to make ends meet.

'Sometimes I wish she would and take Antony with her,' he added, almost meaning it. 'I could use a decent night's sleep!'

'You'd miss her dreadfully,' Melissa said, smiling,

knowing that he was deeply in love with his pretty wife.

He grinned ruefully. 'Yes, I know. She keeps me sane. I don't really care about the bills or the bad nights or a bloody-minded boss as long as I can always go home to Pamela. Perhaps that's just what Gregory needs—a woman at the end of the day. But he's such a cold-blooded blighter that I can't imagine any woman taking him on. Unless you fancy the job, Melissa? I think you could humanise any man—even our Ben!'

Her face flamed and she wondered if he was being very perceptive or if she had stupidly betrayed the newfound intimacy of her relationship with the SSO in some way. She had tried so hard to be as impersonal as he was. She had crushed her emotions out of the way with a firmness that did credit to her Hartlake training. She had resolutely avoided reminding him by glance or smile or word of all that had happened between them. She had followed his lead against all the instincts of her heart and body—and it was hard that Jamie should now tease her just as if he suspected how she felt about Ben Gregory.

'No, thanks!' she retorted flippantly, in sheer self-defence. 'I like to leave my work behind at the end of the day!'

'He'd be bloody hard work too, I should think.' Jamie sounded wry. 'Does he ever have a pleasant word for anyone, I wonder?'

'I'm off now, Greaves.' The surgeon's tone was cold, cutting, as the words broke into the discussion he had obviously overheard. 'Try not to turn Theatres into a social club in my absence, or you'll discover just how unpleasant I *can* be! I want a careful check kept on that cholecystectomy over the weekend, by the way. He's still very jaundiced.' He turned away, his glance sweeping over Melissa without any apparent liking or warmth.

Past caring what Jamie or anyone else thought, Melissa whisked off her theatre gown and hurried after him out of Theatres. She saw him at the end of the corridor, waiting for the lift.

'B . . . Mr Gregory!' She bit back his first name just in time, conscious of a passing porter.

He looked at her with a slight wariness in his grey eyes and she realised that there had been almost a challenge in the way she said his name. She was instantly cross with herself. She mustn't seem to be making demands on him, taking their relationship for granted. She mustn't throw herself at him. He didn't owe her anything whatever her foolish heart might feel!

'Not now, Nurse,' he said coolly. 'I'm in a hurry.'

It was an unmistakable snub. Melissa was chilled, dismayed. 'It doesn't matter,' she said carefully, with pride, hoping the hurt didn't show as she forced a smile. 'It really isn't important . . .'

'So I gathered.' It was curt, cryptic.

She instantly took his meaning. He had overheard that conversation with Jamie, taken exception to the impulsive and empty words that she had spoken. Before she could protest that they had only been meant as a smokescreen to protect them both from gossip, he stepped into the lift as the doors were closing.

She walked slowly back to Theatres. It scarcely seemed possible that the stranger with ice in his eyes and voice could be the same man who had held her and kissed her and turned her world upside down with the potency of his lovemaking. He had been keeping her at a cool distance all day as if stressing that a casual encounter left no claim on either of them. Now he was annoyed, and she was troubled that he hadn't allowed her to explain. But it was so difficult to indulge in private conversation in a busy hospital with the constant to and fro of staff and patients. It had been foolish to try, she admitted. *Not now*, he had said with brusque impatience. She must simply wait for the moment to be right.

Despite her dismay, she decided to take heart from his obvious resentment and irritation that she had been talking him over with Jamie with apparent malice. She knew she mustn't snatch at straws but oh! how she hoped that he cared enough to be just a little hurt. She would make it up to him so gladly! She wanted desperately to believe that this was a beginning rather than the end that she had been dreading all day. She couldn't bear to wonder if Ben had merely needed her, used her and then regretted that they had become involved at all. Deep down, she felt it was much too likely . . .

'Did you manage to catch up with our Ben?'

Melissa mustered a smile to dispel the slightly sly amusement in Jamie's eyes. 'Yes. I'd forgotten to give him a message from Sister.' She didn't know or care if he believed her.

'He's off to Bury St Edmunds for the weekend so we can all relax,' Jamie said lightly.

She felt the blood draining from her cheeks with shock. 'Bury St Edmunds . . . ?'

'Cheryl says he's got a girl there so perhaps he isn't such a cold fish, after all.' Jamie grinned. 'Let's hope she'll send him back to us in a happier frame of mind!'

Melissa tried not to flinch away from the thought of him in another woman's arms. 'Did he mention his plans to Cheryl? He isn't usually so forthcoming,' she said, trying to sound casually interested rather than deeply concerned.

'He told me, actually. First thing this morning when he seemed to be in a surprisingly good mood. He turned foul again within minutes, mind you. Didn't you notice?'

Melissa shook her head. She had only noticed his careful impersonality, the complete lack of anything resembling a smile in those grey eyes. 'I expect I'm used to his manner,' she said brightly. 'I work with him all the time, Jamie.'

'I daresay you've never known him any different,' he agreed. 'He's very off-hand with the nurses, isn't he? I came quite near to liking him this morning, though. More to him than meets the eye, I'd say.' He moved towards the door. 'Well, I'm away to the wards if anyone wants me.'

Melissa went into the nurses' changing-room and was thankful to find it empty. She pulled the mob cap from her hair and it tumbled about her face in a pale cloud, soft and shining. She thought of Ben's hands wound in her long hair, drawing her closer to be kissed. She thought of his kiss, and her heart trembled with the terrible fear that she might never know it again.

It seemed that he was rushing to Bury St Edmunds at his first opportunity to claim back the woman he loved from his friend. He would probably succeed, too. For there was so much strength and determination and forceful mastery in him that no woman could resist him if he made up his mind to have her, she thought ruefully.

But she wasn't important enough to drive that other woman from his mind and heart, it seemed. She was just an interlude that he wanted to forget . . .

Going off duty, she emerged into pouring rain to find Neville waiting for her, as they had arranged. She had forgotten all about him and her foolish promise for the future which had raised all his hopes.

But she found a smile for him and he put a fond arm about her shoulders and hurried her into the car against the rain. He snatched a kiss as he turned on the ignition and told her that it was too long since he had seen her.

'Two days!' she exclaimed, laughing at him, not sure whether to be alarmed or touched by the meaningful warmth of his greeting.

'A lot can happen in two days, my love,' he declared lightly.

'Yes,' she agreed carefully. 'I suppose it can . . .' She was thankful that he didn't know just how much had happened to her since she had sent him away after that extravagant night out, knowing that he wanted to make love to her and quite determined not to rush into anything that would alter their relationship so irrevocably.

Now she thought wryly that if she had been so ready to tumble into loving and yield her precious virginity without a moment's hesitation, it was possibly a pity that she hadn't chosen Neville, who was so dear and familiar and trusted, instead of a man who offered nothing for the future because he had nothing to give her. But it seemed that loving wasn't a matter of choice but of destiny . . .

As Neville's car was about to pull away from the hospital, a white Mercedes shot past them at speed.

Melissa caught a glimpse of a stony-faced driver and with a shock of dismay she wondered if Ben could have been waiting for her.

Not now, he had said. Had he meant only that he would talk to her in the very near future, away from the restrictions of hospital surroundings and too many interested eyes and ears? He had known that she was going off duty at about the same time as himself, had he planned to spend some time with her before he left for Bury St Edmunds? Had he intended to explain his sudden departure from the flat, his coolness of the morning, the motives that took him to see his ex-fiancée again?

Had he seen Neville's welcoming warmth, that proprietary arm about her shoulders, her own apparent response to a lover's greeting? If so, coming on top of her remarks to Jamie that she hadn't had time to explain away, he might feel that she was as unaffected by their brief encounter as himself and could dismiss it just as easily.

It might salve her pride if he came back to Baymouth to tell her that he had rescued his engagement. But it did absolutely nothing for her heart and its very foolish hopes . . .

It was dreadful to take Neville into the flat and remember Ben's overwhelming presence and all that had happened there. She felt as if every room must be stamped with the impression of that powerful and heady passion. She didn't want Neville to touch her, to kiss her, to blur the memory of Ben's lovemaking, with his lips and the urgency of his body.

'You're edgy, darling,' he said when she had retreated

from him for the third time with the flimsiest of excuses. 'Come and be kissed . . . relax!'

'Not now . . .' Echoing Ben's words, his image filled her mind and heart and body with sudden longing.

'Now,' Neville insisted. He moved to put his arms round her and smiled into her wary eyes. 'I've thought of nothing else but you since I left you the other night, Melissa. I've been in love before but never like this . . . I want you so much . . .'

'We agreed to take things slowly,' she reminded him a little desperately, lacking the heart to push him away although she was frozen in his embrace. If he felt only a fraction of the ache in her heart for Ben and the longing to be loved that she knew, then she could only feel an overwhelming compassion and a deep regret that his cousinly and casual affection had turned into an intense and demanding need.

He sighed. 'This *is* slow for me,' he told her ruefully. 'I don't think I've ever waited two days for a woman to make up her mind if she wants me or not! My irresistible charm usually gets me what I want when I want it!'

Melissa believed him. Like most men, he was an opportunist who took what he could when and where he could. Finer feelings such as loving evidently didn't enter into the matter. Why should she suppose that it was any different for Ben, strongly sensual and capable of an urgent and exciting and very potent passion?

He loved that girl in Bury St Edmunds, had hoped and planned and waited to marry her for four years. In the meantime, he had probably enjoyed fleeting sexual encounters with other women from time to time that meant nothing at all to him but the satisfaction of a normal need. It didn't lessen him in his own or anyone else's eyes. Men were expected to sow their wild oats before they settled down, after all.

A man seemed to give only his body in the physical act of love. While a woman gave so much of herself—even if she didn't love the man who held and caressed and delighted her. But Melissa was very much in love . . .

CHAPTER SIX

WITH Neville's ardent arms about her, Melissa suffered his kisses, the tentative caress of her reluctant breasts, the longing in the way that he held her. He couldn't help but sense her tension and her instinctive withdrawal from the merest hint of passion.

He sighed. 'I seem to be losing my touch,' he said wryly, at last.

'No. It's me,' she said quickly, careful of his pride. 'I'm sorry . . .'

He drew her to sit beside him on the sofa, sliding an arm about her shoulders in an embrace that wasn't a threat. 'Tell me what's wrong. Don't you trust me?'

'Of course I do.'

'Then what is it? The other girls in my life? I'll get rid of them all,' he promised. 'I only want you, anyway.'

'Greater love hath no man,' Melissa teased gently but her heart was heavy. He was very dear to her and she had never heard that particular note in his voice or seen that particular look in his eyes before and it troubled her. If she had never known and loved Ben, she might be thrilled and delighted that this golden lad, this darling of the gods, had suddenly decided to love and want her to the exclusion of every other woman. Now she could only be sad.

He turned her face to him. 'I'm not expecting to be the first if that's what bothers you,' he said frankly. 'You aren't sweet sixteen any more and you're too lovely not to have had the men buzzing about you for years. With my track record, I'm in no position to mind.'

Melissa said nothing. She shouldn't lie to him but she couldn't possibly tell him the truth, either. Only yesterday, she could have indignantly refuted that easy assumption that she was no longer a virgin, she thought ruefully. How hurt he would be if he knew that she had sent him away with a firm *no* only to melt into another man's arms as if she had belonged in them for ever.

Neville obviously drew his own conclusions from her silence. He touched his lips to her brow, very tender. 'I do love you, Melissa . . .'

She sighed. 'I love you, too,' she told him carefully. 'But not in the way that you mean. I can't help it, Neville. I wish I could.'

'There's plenty of time.' He hugged her affectionately. 'Everything's in my favour, after all. Just stop thinking of me as Cousin Neville and try to imagine me as the man you could marry if you play your cards right.'

She glanced at him swiftly, startled. Then she saw the engaging twinkle in his eyes and she relaxed and laughed. 'So that's the carrot you dangle in front of all your girlfriends,' she reproached him.

'It works,' he said, smiling.

'I bet it does. But I've known you rather too long,' she said dryly. 'I don't think you'll ever marry. You'd hate being tied down to one woman.'

'Depends on the woman . . .' He brushed her lips with his own, very lightly. Then that fleeting touch became an urgent kiss, dispelling laughter. 'Darling . . . oh, darling! Don't disappoint me when I want you so,' he begged.

Melissa was thankful that she didn't feel the slightest response to his passion. It would have seemed a betrayal of Ben and the wonderful world she had known in his arms. At the same time, she was sorry that she was so cold and unresponsive, hurting and disappointing Neville.

Neville was persuaded to take no for an answer, fortunately. He shrugged off his disappointment and resigned himself to waiting and hoping, and didn't reproach her by word or look or deed—and she loved him for it. Just as she had always loved him. A mingling of admiration and amusement and tender affection, utterly untouched by physical attraction.

His feeling for her was very physical and she didn't mean to be fooled into believing that he was truly in love with her. Just now, he wanted to believe it, she felt. Like her friend, Vicki, he enjoyed falling in and out of love and found so much excitement in the pursuit of a new conquest. It was just a light-hearted fun thing for him, she thought wryly, knowing that loving was a once in a lifetime experience for herself.

Loving Ben, longing for him, Melissa hoped with all her heart that the night she had spent in his arms wouldn't turn out to be a once in a lifetime experience, too . . .

She was on duty the following day and the hours in Theatres seemed long and anxious and rather empty without the chance of seeing Ben who was off until Monday. She wondered how she would get through the weekend, aching to see him again, needing to know if she was of any importance at all in his life, dreading to hear that he had persuaded the girl in Bury St Edmunds to marry him after all. She didn't doubt that was his mission.

It was very quiet in Theatres. There were no operations on the list for that day and no emergencies for the duty surgeon to deal with.

Melissa spent much of the day checking equipment and supplies and organising a thorough scrub and sterilising process of everything that was used in the vital business of surgery.

She found plenty to do but she wasn't busy enough, obviously. For she still had too much time to think about Ben and to remember the heaven of his embrace and the hurt in the way he had held her at arms' length only the next day. She scolded herself for being so helplessly, so foolishly and so inexplicably in love with a man who probably hadn't given her a thought since he left St Biddulph's for his weekend off duty.

She hadn't slept very well, having too much on her mind and too many reminders of the previous night. She had little appetite and she only picked indifferently at the excellent lunch that was served in the nurses' dining-room. In her mind's eye, she kept seeing Ben's tall figure and burnished head, and that sudden smile with its rare, heart-stopping enchantment. In her mind's ear, she kept hearing the unexpected tenderness in the way he had said her name, turning it into an endearment—but it was marred by the echo of a cool, rather sardonic voice saying *Not now, nurse* as though she was in unwelcome pursuit of a man who had already tired of her.

Vicki carried her tray from the servery and joined Melissa. 'Hi!'

Melissa tried to look pleased to see her friend but she wasn't really in the mood to be sociable. 'Hallo, Vicki . . .'

Vicki looked at her closely as she sat down. The warm brown eyes saw rather more than people imagined for she had a reputation for sailing happily through life without a care for anyone's problems but her own, and they were very few.

'You're looking wan. Rushed off your feet in Theatres?'

'No. We're very quiet, thank heavens. It gives us a chance to catch up on our routines. I'm not very popular with the juniors just now, I've got them scrubbing everything in sight!'

'Darling, you're turning that lettuce leaf over as though you expect to find an unidentified alien object!' Vicki declared lightly.

Melissa laughed, laid down her fork. 'I'm not very hungry.'

'Too hot to eat—or just in love?' It was teasing but direct.

'Being in love never seems to affect *your* appetite, I've noticed,' she returned, adroitly fencing.

Vicki smiled. 'That's true,' she agreed. She never minded being teased about her fickle and light-hearted dealings with a variety of men. 'I usually eat like a horse to keep up my strength.' The brown eyes were merry, mischievous. 'I'm looking for someone to love at the moment now that Paul's turned out to be such a disappointment,' she went on lightly. 'I did have my eye on the SSO but I hear that he's disappeared. You haven't done away with him, I suppose?'

Melissa raised an eyebrow. 'Why would I want to?' It was slightly defensive. She didn't quite trust that seeming innocence in her friend's bantering tone. Like every hospital, St Biddulph's had a very efficient grapevine that was not always as accurate as it might be. A chance word exchanged with Ben, an unguarded expression, could be blown up out of all proportion in no time at all. She suspected that Vicki was probing, very gently.

'To get him off your back, of course. You weren't liking him very much earlier in the week and I hear that he's been making your life a misery in Theatres.'

'You hear so much that I'm surprised you don't know that he's gone away for the weekend,' Melissa said, rather tartly.

'That's a nuisance.' Vicki seemed deaf to that hint of impatience and irritation. 'I thought he could take me to the dance tomorrow night. I know there'll be plenty of men there to keep me happy but it isn't like having someone special, is it?'

Once a month, the hospital League of Friends arranged a dance for the staff that was always well attended. This month, the date happened to coincide with Vicki's birthday and a group of her friends meant to help her to celebrate it in style. Until a few days before she had planned to be there with the current boyfriend. Now, having quarrelled and broken off with Paul, she was looking for someone to take his place . . . in more ways than one.

Melissa wasn't surprised that her friend seemed so sure of annexing Ben's attention if he had been available

that weekend. Vicki seemed to have a gift for getting any
man she wanted. Ben might have been in the mood to
notice someone as pretty and as amusing and as undemanding as Vicki, too. All that week he had been in the
right frame of mind to console his hurt in the arms of any
woman who seemed willing. Melissa thought heavily
that it was probably the merest chance that he had
picked on her, and his subsequent indifference came
close to convincing her that she had been a disappointment. Vicki wasn't promiscuous but she probably had
much more experience than herself in satisfying the
sexual needs of a very sensual man.

'He doesn't seem to be your type,' she said, as lightly
as she could.

'Oh, I don't know. There's something about our
strong, silent and very sexy SSO that appeals to me,'
Vicki mused, smiling. 'It isn't just those fantastic good
looks, either. It might be the challenge of a man who
doesn't seem to like women very much, I suppose. What
do you think?'

'I haven't given it a thought.' Melissa hastily re-
deemed the snap in her voice by adding with a smile, 'It's
probably the challenge of a man who didn't seem to like
you the other day. I suspect that it put you on your
mettle!' She rose from the table. 'I must get back . . .'

'What about you, Melissa?' Vicki detained her with a
light hand on her arm.

'Me?' It was sharp. 'He doesn't appeal to me!'

'That isn't what I meant . . .' Vicki was a little surprised by that forceful denial. 'Who's taking you to the
dance?'

'Oh!' Melissa felt her face flame as she realised the

betrayal of that swift and quite unnecessary lie. 'Neville. My cousin.' she said hastily.

Vicki nodded, pleased. She had met and liked Neville. 'You're seeing a lot of him lately. Is that getting serious?' she asked.

'Neville's like you. He doesn't take anyone or anything seriously,' Melissa told her lightly and escaped.

It wasn't true. Neville was taking their relationship much too seriously and it troubled her that he seemed to be really in love for the first time in his life. Why her, she wondered wryly—and why now? Had something blossomed in her since Ben came to St Biddulph's to stir her heart and senses even before she knew it . . . something that had quickened Neville to a new and unexpected awareness of her as a woman?

At the end of the day's work, Melissa caught a bus into Baymouth and collected her car from the garage, trying not to wince too obviously at the size of the repair bill. About to head for home, she impulsively turned off on the coast road for Spelby. She knew it was probably madness but no one could say for sure that Ben had gone to Bury St Edmunds for the weekend. He might have changed his mind and decided that it would be a waste of time and effort. He might have felt that he didn't want to mend his broken engagement after all. If he was on his own in that dreadful bungalow and feeling lonely, he might be glad to see her, she told herself with rather forlorn hope.

Perhaps it was throwing herself at his head. Melissa didn't care. There didn't seem to be much room for pride in a heart that swelled with love and longing and need for the one man in the world who really mattered and always would. She was missing Ben dreadfully. Just as if he had always been in her life. She hadn't known that loving could be so painful and demanding, so insistent in searching for the smallest crumb of comfort, she thought wryly, clinging to the hope that he would be home and welcoming and no longer the coldly impersonal surgeon who had snubbed her so hurtfully.

Spelby was crowded with holidaymakers from the nearby caravan camp. Children clambered over the dunes and shovelled sand into buckets, filling the air with their shouts and laughter while their parents relaxed over drinks in the pub garden or strolled on the beach and over the cliffs on the sunny summer evening.

Melissa had trouble in squeezing her small car into a parking space. There was no sign of a white Mercedes and she realised that she had come on a fool's errand. If Ben wasn't away then he was certainly out for the evening. Her heart sank but she still walked through the dunes to the sheltered cluster of holiday bungalows, attracting some attention in her nurse's uniform.

His was closed up, deserted, looking as though it hadn't been lived in for months. Melissa could have cried with disappointment.

She sat down on the wooden steps for a few minutes, almost as if she expected him to come striding along the beach towards her, tall and very distinctive with that proud, handsome head and the powerful build, dearer than any man ought to be on the strength of a few weeks of working together and one enchanted night of love.

Disconsolate, she drove home. When she reached the flat, she could hear the shrill summons of the telephone through the thin front door. She was in a panic to find her

key and let herself in before it stopped ringing. She
rushed across the room and picked up the receiver. 'Ben
. . . ?' she said foolishly, quite breathless, much too
eager. The dialling tone was the only response. She
hadn't been quite quick enough to answer and the caller
had rung off. She was dismayed until she realised that
Ben probably didn't even know the number.

Why would he ring her, anyway? If he was interested
in her, if he cared anything at all for her, he wouldn't
have rushed away that weekend without even trying to
see her. He must know that she was desperate for a
word, a smile, some small hope for the future, Melissa
told herself bleakly.

She ought to be angry with him. She ought to despise a
man who could make love to her with such potent
passion and then ignore her as though she was nothing in
his life. Certainly she ought not to love him so much that
her life promised to revolve about hopes and dreams of
him until the end of time.

Why on earth didn't she put him out of her heart and
mind and give more thought to Neville, who did care
about her and was anxious to prove it in every possible
way? There couldn't be any future for her in loving Ben,
while Neville was very loving, very attentive, trying so
hard to be patient and to understand her resistance and
her reluctance.

Why didn't she simply open her arms and her heart to
him and hope that his ardour and his tender affection
could erase the memory of another man? Why didn't she
sensibly concentrate all her energies on loving him and
think seriously about marrying him, and forget the
foolish dream of spending her life with a cold, hard and

insensitive surgeon who might be destined to remain a bachelor?

On a sudden impulse, she reached for the telephone and dialled the Maresby number. Anyone might have answered. Her aunt or uncle. One of the girls. By chance, it was Neville himself and his voice warmed so instantly in delight that she couldn't regret the blurted invitation to spend the evening at the flat with her. He assured her that he would be with her as soon as possible.

Melissa wondered if she was about to burn all her bridges—and if it mattered so very much, after all. For all Ben knew, or apparently cared, there had been a dozen men before him and there might be a dozen to follow, she thought, rather bitterly. The precious gift of her virginity had meant as little to him as the eager giving of her heart—and he had seemed to be as unaware of the one as the other, she thought, torn between relief and regret.

For reasons of his own, Neville didn't even try to take advantage of the opportunity she had offered. Relieved by the lack of demand in his kiss and the reassurance in his manner during a pleasant evening, like those of previous days when he hadn't even thought of loving her, she felt a warmth and affection for him that might easily have turned into loving with time if she had never known Ben and thrilled to his lovemaking.

She didn't know if Neville had given up hope or lost interest, or was merely resisting the temptation to make love to her. But he was very much friend and cousin rather than would-be lover that evening, until he eventually rose to leave her just before midnight. Then he reached for her and kissed her, very gently, very controlled, but with a hint of the longing that he obviously felt for her.

He smiled into her eyes and there was loving tenderness in the way he looked, the way he kissed her again with lips that yearned to linger.

'I have been good, haven't I?' he said softly, pressing his cheek to her shining hair.

'Very good,' she agreed, smiling, hugging him impulsively.

'Don't think it's been easy.' He sounded rueful. 'I'm not the most patient man in the world and I want you terribly. But I'm determined not to rush you into something you might regret. It means far too much to me. *You* mean too much, Melissa. I'm sure that you love me, and I'm prepared to wait until you're sure too.'

She knew that he wasn't as confident as he sounded. Neville had always been so sure of himself in the past. She was responsible for that unfamiliar and rather touching uncertainty and it made her wonder if he really did love her as much as he claimed. He might be more serious than she suspected when he spoke of marriage.

'And if it never happens?' She was gentle, preparing him for possible disappointment. 'What if I just can't love you in the way you want?'

She heard the swift, sharp intake of his breath. Then he shrugged, smiled. 'Oh, I won't do anything silly, love,' he said with quick, light-hearted reassurance. 'I won't shoot myself or join the foreign legion. I'm not the type. I'll just look round for another girl who can love me and try not to think about what a great life we might have had together.'

Her heart moved as she kissed him goodnight with soft, sweet lips and hoped that she wouldn't have to hurt him in the end. She had never wanted him to love her. She still found it hard to believe that her handsome, carefree cousin with the long string of girlfriends could be in earnest about someone as ordinary as herself. She was nothing like the lovely and sophisticated and probably sexually experienced girls that he usually admired and pursued. But that might be just the reason why he wanted her, Melissa thought shrewdly.

She wondered how it was that he hadn't sensed her readiness to say yes to him if he had tried to persuade her into bed that night. For she didn't seem to have the heart to go on refusing something that would make him happy and didn't really make any difference to her, any more. Her virginity was gone for ever, after all.

But Neville hadn't even tried to make love to her. He knew that she wasn't sure about such a final and irrevocable commitment and he also knew that it was vital to the future of their relationship that she should be sure. For nothing would ever be the same between them if cousins and friends became lovers as he wished.

He was really very dear to her. For the first time Melissa understood how it was possible for a woman to marry someone she didn't love and live a lie for the sake of his happiness and peace of mind. She felt that she cared enough about Neville to do that for him, if she could be convinced that he loved her with all his heart and that it would mean his real and lasting contentment—and only if she knew beyond all shadow of a doubt that Ben didn't want her and never would, she hastily qualified.

While there was the slightest smattering of hope that he might forget the woman he had meant to marry when he was in her arms and perhaps even come to love her one day, she wouldn't relinquish her dream.

He would be back at St Biddulph's on Monday and she would know if his trip to Bury St Edmunds had been a success or a disaster. She would know whether she must be glad for his sake that he had regained his happiness or whether to be glad for her own sake that she could still hold out her arms to him.

She meant to confront him at the very first opportunity. She had to know how she stood and if there was any future in loving him. And she was determined that he shouldn't freeze her this time with that cold and forbidding hauteur . . .

CHAPTER SEVEN

THE ONE thing that Melissa particularly liked about working at St Biddulph's was being off duty at weekends. She worked very long hours on the three operating days each week as a regular theatre nurse, but when she came off duty on Friday afternoon she was free until the following Monday.

Sometimes she spent the weekend with Neville's family at Maresby and enjoyed helping out at busy times in the garden centre. Sometimes she drove down to London to look up her friends who were still at Hartlake. Sometimes she visited a friend from her training days who had married a doctor and now lived in Scarborough.

This weekend it was Vicki's birthday and the dance and she spent Saturday afternoon wandering around the shops in Baymouth, trying to forget work and Ben and Neville and everything else that had been dominating her thoughts for days.

Then, crossing the market square, she thought she saw Ben striding along the crowded pavement and she ran to catch him, dodging in and out of bustling shoppers and dawdling holidaymakers, her heart banging against her ribs with painfully eager excitement.

About to catch at Ben's arm, she suddenly saw that the man was a stranger. He stared at her in surprise. Melissa stopped short, feeling foolish. Someone barged into her with a pram. Hastily moving aside, murmuring an apology, she turned to walk slowly back to the supermarket, downcast.

His particular height and build and warm colouring were not so unusual as she had supposed, she thought ruefully. There were a dozen men in Baymouth that day who could have passed as the surgeon from a slight distance. She was an awful fool to be constantly hoping and looking for him when he was miles away in Bury St Edmunds, enjoying the company of his friends and probably mending his broken engagement to his satisfaction . . .

That evening, Vicki was in high spirits and as flirtatious as ever, the pretty and vivacious centre of attraction in a lively, noisy group. In a spirit of mischief, she was flirting with the very good-looking Neville. Melissa thought if further proof of the warmth of his feeling for her if he could resist the lovely and alluring Vicki. So many men fell prey to her pretty face and lively manner and enchanting lightness of heart.

She hadn't told Vicki that her cousin had turned into would-be lover so unexpectedly, reluctant to make it reality by putting it into words. It was all too new to her, even now. In the space of a few hours she had been very sure how she felt about Ben, she knew it might take weeks before she made up her mind what to do about Neville.

She hadn't allowed him to tell his family about the change in his feelings, either. Not yet, she had pleaded. His parents would be delighted and ready to make plans for them both, she knew. They were fond of her and anxious to see their only son settled with an acceptable girl. She didn't want to raise false hopes. She didn't want

Neville to assume that they were set for the intimacy of a lasting love affair.

In fact, she was playing for time until her tumultuous feelings allowed her to know if she could really accept Neville as a substitute for the man she loved.

She was fond of him and she enjoyed his company and she was comfortable with him despite the gentle, insidious pressure that he was putting on her resistance. She knew it would be easy for her to go on saying no to him because she didn't have the slightest temptation to say yes. But it wasn't very fair to him. Soon, she must either relent and let him make love to her or she must make it clear that they could never be lovers.

She wondered if she was clinging to him because she knew in her heart that Ben had nothing to give her, that there was no promise of happiness in loving him and she was sure to need the comfort and the consolation that Neville would be only too glad to offer.

He was very loving and tender that evening and she felt that she probably wouldn't need to tell Vicki of the subtle change in their relationship. He looked and smiled and behaved just like the lover he longed to be and Melissa decided to relax and enjoy the warm affection that surrounded her. It was a kind of balm for the hurt in her heart because another man didn't want to be with her that weekend.

Later in the evening, having almost convinced herself that she wasn't thinking of anyone but Neville or anything but the delight of dancing with him, Melissa was laughing up at him in response to some light-hearted banter when she suddenly saw Ben standing at the bar.

This time it was unmistakably Ben, and her heart

leaped at the sight of him, so unexpected. The lighting above the bar turned his bronze head to gleaming gold and heightened the sensual attraction of his handsome face. He was a very striking and impressive man with a strength and a magnetism that surely few women could resist, she thought, wistfully.

'There's your friend,' Neville said, a little dryly, as he whirled her past the surgeon to the music.

'He isn't exactly a friend,' she said carefully.

'He doesn't seem to be anyone's friend,' Neville returned with a touch of malice.

Melissa had also observed that people seemed to be leaving him severely alone. The staff of St Biddulph's were usually a very friendly crowd which proved that he hadn't made himself popular in his first weeks as SSO and that some of his colleagues were still smarting from the lash of that caustic tongue.

She wondered what had brought him back so much earlier than she had dared to hope. Perhaps it hadn't been a successful or satisfying trip. Her heart might ache for his disappointment but it couldn't help filling with hope for her own sake.

Melissa was more distinctive than she knew in the crowded ballroom, with her pale, shining hair and lovely, laughing face and the soft rose of her chiffon frock that swirled as her equally blond partner swung her round with a flourish at the end of their dance. Breathless, she clung to his arm as they walked from the dance floor. She looked directly into Ben's enigmatic eyes as he turned to watch them on their way back to the table.

He raised his glass to his lips in a gesture that might or might not have been a toast. She smiled at him uncertainly. In return, she received the briefest of unsmiling nods before he turned back to the bar. Her heart lurched in dismay. Love and longing for him melted her very bones but if he was determined to treat her like a stranger, what could she do?

As she sat down, Vicki touched her arm and nodded at the surgeon. 'The love of your life just walked in,' she joked. 'Looking as grim as ever! Perhaps you ought to go over and cheer him up, Melissa. He might even like to join the party.'

'Maybe he would,' she returned brightly. 'I'll go and ask him!' She smiled at Vicki just as though she thought it all a great joke, too. 'Why don't you and Neville dance this one and I'll see if I can organise another birthday present for you. I know you fancy him!' It was light-hearted enough to allay anyone's suspicions of her readiness to seize on Vicki's suggestion, she felt.

'Ben Gregory on a plate would round off the day very nicely, I must admit,' Vicki agreed, her brown eyes dancing. 'I don't care if he does have a nasty tongue. Who wants conversation from a man who looks that good, anyway?'

Having little choice in the matter but not appearing to mind too much, Neville took Vicki on to the dance floor. Melissa watched them for a few moments, trying to nerve herself to approach someone who was looking particularly unapproachable, keeping his back carefully turned to their corner of the ballroom.

He didn't seem to know that she was beside him until she touched him lightly on the arm. 'Hallo, Ben . . . nice to see you.' She tried hard to sound casual, merely friendly. It came out as sheer desperation tinged with resentment, she thought ruefully.

He glanced at her briefly. Dedicated to his work, proud of his success, ambitious for his future, Ben hadn't planned to marry for years. Then Delia had persuaded him, against his better judgment, to become engaged, to make wedding plans, and had made a fool of him in consequence. He was more angry with himself for a weakness that was totally out of character than with Delia for preferring to marry someone else.

Proud, still sensitive, still angry and inclined to be wary of further involvement with any woman, he told himself not to overlook the obvious fact that Melissa was a flirt and probably even a wanton. Scarcely knowing her, it might not have been wise for him to go so eagerly in search of her that evening, heart and body stirring at the thought of her. Now, seeing her radiance, her response to her partner, her obvious enjoyment of the evening with someone else, he knew he had been a fool to allow himself to think of her so tenderly.

'You seem to be enjoying the evening,' he said in a clipped, cold response that relegated her to the position of stranger and eclipsed the warm intimacy that they had shared.

The curt tone and his obvious indifference smote Melissa to the heart. But she still smiled. 'Hey!' she reproached, trying for lightness. 'Remember me! I'm a friend!'

'They're rather thin on the ground at present,' he returned dryly. 'Perhaps I ought to buy you a drink.'

'Are you smiling inside?' she asked brightly, just as if he hadn't shrivelled her with that sardonic retort. 'Because it isn't showing on the outside!' Her own smile felt as though it was pinned to her lips and she could only hope that it was managing to hide her dismay.

'Why don't you just go back to your partner? He smiles enough for three people.' It was caustic. A nerve throbbed in his jaw.

Pain welled. Tears suddenly pricked at the back of her eyes. He didn't want her at all. He was making it very plain and he was breaking her heart, and there was nothing she could do about it, she thought heavily.

But she had to try. Pride wasn't as important as her need of him. '*You* should smile more often,' she told him warmly. 'It suits you . . .' She tucked her hand into his arm, hoping the small gesture of intimacy would remind him, soften him, chase the coldness from those grey eyes. 'If you're buying me a drink it's a Martini,' she added, still smiling, refusing to be rebuffed.

She was hurling herself at him quite blatantly, but she couldn't let him thrust her away. He was her only chance of real happiness and she was so sure in her heart that they were meant to love each other.

Ben looked down at the hand that rested on his arm. Melissa thought there was a little glow of anger in his eyes and her heart shook. She remembered how scornfully he had spoken of girls who had pursued him in the past. Did he despise her, too? Did he feel that she had been too easy, too eager? Was she making a fool of herself now by refusing to be brushed off by his obvious lack of interest or warmth?

He caught the barman's eye and ordered her drink. Melissa didn't want it but it gave her an excuse to linger at the bar with him. Vicki and Neville were still dancing and getting on so well that they weren't taking a scrap of notice of her efforts to soften the stony-faced surgeon. But she sensed that others were watching and speculating about their relationship.

'I didn't expect to see you here,' she told him. 'Someone said you were away for the weekend.' Carefully she tried not to let it sound like a reproach because she had heard it second-hand.

'So I was. I went to Bury to straighten out a few things. It didn't take as long as I expected.'

As he reached to pick up his glass, Melissa saw that the knuckles of his right hand were skinned and she knew that he had yielded to a passion of a very different kind while he was away. She wondered if it had helped to exorcise that terrible anger in him, still simmering beneath the surface.

'I hope you straightened them out to your satisfaction,' she said quietly. 'Otherwise it was a pity to have risked your hands.'

He followed her glance. 'Oh, that! A slight difference of opinion between friends . . . over rights,' he said, very dry.

Melissa's heart was high in her throat as she said carefully; 'Did you win?'

Sardonic humour gleamed suddenly in the deep-set eyes. 'No. I conceded victory to the other fellow because I decided that I didn't want the prize, after all.'

Hearing only pride, Melissa didn't realise all that was behind that wry admission. Her heart went out to him. She longed to hold him, comfort him, give him ease for his obvious torment of mind and heart and body. He *had* tried to get back the woman he loved, without success, it seemed. She wondered how any woman could fail to love him, to want him, to hold on to him with both hands for the happiness he could give.

She traced a pattern in a little spillage on the bar counter where her drink had been put down too sharply by a rushed barman. 'So you came back early?'

'There was nothing to keep me in Bury,' he said carelessly. 'And something that I wanted in Baymouth.'

She didn't even dare to wonder if he could mean herself with those light, cryptic words. He was a proud man but surely he wouldn't hesitate to tell her frankly if he wanted her. It was too unlikely—his whole attitude to her was so hurtful and discouraging that if she had an ounce of pride she would walk away and never speak to him again except when the circumstances of working with him in Theatres forced it upon her.

She drank a little of the Martini and wondered why she didn't seem to have any pride at all where he was concerned.

'Well, I'm glad to see you.' She smiled at him. 'You went off in such a rush the other day and I wanted to talk to you. I wondered why you left the flat so early without even waking me. I expect it sounds silly but I didn't like you leaving so abruptly.' It took all her courage to talk of something that he seemed intent on forgetting as quickly as possible.

He glanced at her with a hint of impatience in his grey eyes. 'I thought you'd realise that I wanted to move the car before morning. It's a distinctive car and it was advertising the fact that I'd stayed the night. I expect your neighbours take an interest in your affairs and I didn't want them talking about you. Some of them work at the hospital, too, don't they?'

'Oh!' Such a simple explanation hadn't occurred to her. She was surprised that he had been so concerned for her reputation—perhaps he had been merely thinking of his own. 'That was thoughtful . . .'

'I can be thoughtful,' It was dry. 'You should get to know me, Melissa.'

Oddly, she felt reproached by something in his tone. Just as if she had been keeping *him* at a distance instead of the other way round. 'I'm trying,' she said quickly, defensively. 'You don't make it easy!' It was impulsive, candid. 'I don't know where I am with you!'

Someone jostled her in trying to reach the busy bar counter and she was thrust against the surgeon. Instantly, Ben put a protective arm about her, surprising her, flooding her with delight and that tingling excitement. He looked down at her flushed and startled face and his arm tightened abruptly, drawing her close.

'That depends on where you want to be,' he said brusquely. 'You always seem to have that damned fellow in tow!'

This was so unexpected that her heart leaped with sudden, quickening hope. 'Neville! You don't have to be jealous of Neville!' she exclaimed.

He frowned. 'That's too strong a word. I just don't like him hanging round you and getting in the way of what I want.'

Melissa could sense the passion flowing in this strongly sensual man who held her against him in an exciting reminder of lovemaking that had swept her over the edge of loving. Her body was melting before the heat in him and her heart was desperately seeking the smallest sign of love in the way he looked and spoke and caught her close. But her level head insisted that sex was all that he had in mind where she was concerned and that she ought to put an end to their very dangerous relationship here and now. For he would take all that she had to give without a thought for the consequences and he would probably break her heart without ever risking his own.

'I'm not sure what it is that you *do* want, Ben,' she said quietly, carefully, searching the intent grey eyes that held her own. But she *was* sure—painfully sure—and her heart cried out in protest that the man she loved should be so unworthy of that loving.

'Just the same as you,' he told her bluntly. 'Don't let's fool ourselves and cloud the issue with unnecessary sentiment. We're adult enough to recognise just what we want from each other and we don't have to complicate a really good relationship by dragging love into it, surely? I've had enough of love to last me a long time!'

Deeply hurt by the blatant words that ripped all the camouflage from a naked sexual need, Melissa pulled herself free of the embrace that was a deliberate and shocking reminder of shared passion.

'Don't cheapen me!' she exclaimed in instinctive, dismayed protest at an attitude that took the warm enchantment of that night and turned it into a casual, promiscuous encounter without even the promise of love to enrich it. Hurt and humiliated, she felt that she could never let him touch her again.

His eyes narrowed abruptly. 'How can the truth cheapen you? Lies certainly would. I won't say that I love you when I don't, Melissa. I've too much respect for you to use such tactics and I don't think they're necessary. I think you want me as much as I want you.'

She felt sick. She knew she had invited this careless confidence by foolishly offering him encouragement in the first place and by her apparent pursuit this evening. But she couldn't bear his casual acceptance of the precious gift of her virginity and his utter failure to appreciate that she had been prompted by the belief that she loved him, not just by the excitement that he knew just how to kindle in a woman. How dared he suppose that she was just as amoral as himself!

'No,' she said proudly. 'You're mistaken. I *don't* want you, Ben. I never did—not really. I was just . . . sorry for you!' She was glad that the lie sounded convincing even to her own ears. Seeing his mouth harden and a little blaze of angry fire in his eyes, she knew that she had struck at his pride just as she had intended. He had trampled her own in the mud without hesitation, after all.

He looked down at her, very intent. Then a sardonic smile twisted his sensual mouth and he said lightly, 'You're very honest. Well, I need some more of your particular brand of sympathy and I thought I could rely on you to provide it. I knew you'd be at this affair. I came back from Bury with the sole purpose of finding you and spending the night with you. That's honest, too, isn't it?'

'Yes,' she said with a gasp, fighting tears. Her chin tilted. 'So honest that it tells me exactly what you think of me—and I wonder why I ever tried to like you!'

She left him, feeling bruised and shaken and despairing, hurrying to the comfort and the kindliness of Neville, who loved her as the surgeon never could for he was entirely without heart. He wanted her for only one thing and had said so, bluntly, insulting her, rejecting all that she had been so ready to give him.

How could she have been so stupid, so easily swept off her feet by a man's physical attractions, so deceived into endowing him with all the qualities that he obviously didn't possess? How could she have been so foolish as to believe that she loved him?

Neville and Vicki had their heads together, chatting like old friends. Vicki was radiant, sparkling. It would have been quite impossible for any red-blooded male to look at her and not feel a stirring of admiration or a spark of attraction.

Not even noticing a little self-consciousness in the way they separated on her arrival, Melissa somehow found a smile from somewhere as she sat down between them.

'Well? What happened to my birthday present?' Vicki demanded brightly.

Melissa looked blank. Then she remembered that light-hearted promise to her friend. 'No luck,' she said, rather stiffly. 'I couldn't persuade him to join the party . . .' She hadn't even tried, she realised. For everything but loving and wanting had gone out of her head as soon as she reached Ben's side. Now, she never wanted to see or speak to him agan.

Vicki shook her head in amused reproach. 'It's a gift,' she declared. 'You have to let a man know that he's wanted, Melissa—without being too obvious. I'll show you how it's done . . .' Smiling, confident, she rose and wove her way through the tables to where Ben still stood.

No casual observer could have realised that Vicki

scarcely knew the surgeon from watching the easy,
confident way that she went up to him, spoke and smiled
and indicated her group of friends, took him by the arm
and brought him across to join them, quite unresist-
ing.

'I think you probably know everyone,' she said airily,
waving a vague hand around the party.

'Not as well as I should, perhaps . . .' It was rather
rueful, calculated to charm. So was the warm, enchanting smile that he bestowed on the group before he sat
down and began to talk to Vicki with unmistakable
admiration and flattering interest.

Melissa almost didn't believe the way he was looking
at her pretty friend, smiling with warm and very attractive friendliness, setting out to charm as he had never
done in all his weeks at St Biddulph's. Was it Vicki's
influence—or a proud attempt to prove that he didn't
need her sympathy or her liking or her friendship?

Her heart contracted painfully as she watched him
with Vicki. She hastily reminded her heart that she
wanted nothing more to do with him and didn't care
how readily he responded to her friend or any other
woman.

She reached for Neville's hand, leaned against his
shoulder and smiled into his eyes, and carefully didn't
look at Ben. He only had eyes for Vicki, anyway—and
she was delighting in the fact that she had succeeded so
easily where Melissa had apparently failed. It was all the
sweeter because he had snubbed her first overture of
friendship, of course. Vicki wasn't exactly spoiled but
she was used to being much admired and much in
demand and getting any man that she happened to want.

Now, it amused her to flirt with the SSO and he seemed only too willing to oblige her.

Melissa could understand her friend's fascination with this very attractive man but she absolutely refused to watch while Vicki set out to captivate him with the coquettish vivacity that men seemed to admire so much . . .

CHAPTER EIGHT

Dancing again with Neville, Melissa was just as encouraging as she knew how to be in the hope that Ben would notice the warm intimacy of their relationship and understand just how unimportant he really was to her.

He swept past them with Vicki in his arms and she saw that he only had eyes for her friend. Her foolish heart lurched in swift, painful resentment that any other woman should be moving in his arms to the sensual rhythm of the music. He was holding Vicki much too close and obviously saying all the things that a woman likes to hear even if she doesn't believe them. Things that he had never said to her, Melissa thought unhappily.

But she hadn't had to be coaxed and cajoled into surrender. She had been more than ready to let him make love to her and she had only herself to blame that he despised her for it. No man valued what was too readily given, after all.

Vicki had her arms wound about Ben's neck and her body pressed invitingly close to him, she was smiling into his eyes with feminine allure and an obvious satisfaction in her conquest of yet another man. If only it had been any other man, Melissa thought bleakly, torn to shreds by an absurd but undeniable jealousy.

He couldn't know how he hurt her with that open pursuit of another woman, disregarding her feelings and any claim she might feel she had on his attention and interest. She thanked heaven he didn't know just how near she had come to making an absolute fool of herself by declaring that she loved him.

She didn't, of course.

It was an absurd infatuation which she could overcome if she put her mind to it, she told herself firmly. It was just a foolish physical attraction, a need he had evoked without even trying and then swiftly turned to his own advantage. He was that kind of man. He hadn't cared if she was a virgin or not. He had just taken what he wanted in a flame of passion. If she hadn't protested and refused and rejected him, he would have gone on taking until he tired of her. Taking everything without giving anything in return.

Neville looked after the dancing couple, too. If Melissa had been in the mood to notice she might have been disconcerted by the look in his very blue eyes and tempted to exclaim wryly *et tu, Brute*!

'I guess I was wrong about your doctor friend,' he said slowly. 'It isn't you that he fancies, after all. It's Vicki. But what was he saying to you at the bar, love? You came back looking quite cross and I don't think you were too pleased when Vicki insisted on bringing him over.'

Melissa smiled, shrugged. 'I told you that I don't like him.' It wasn't a lie. Liking had little to do with the way she felt about the surgeon. 'He doesn't like me, either.' That must be only too true, she thought heavily, remembering the painful bluntness of the words that hadn't given a thought for her feelings. Liking had nothing to do with what he wanted from her! 'It isn't surprising that I couldn't talk him into joining us.' She added, very light, 'Vicki's welcome to him. I'd much rather have you!'

There was the merest fraction of hesitation before he smiled into her eyes and said, rather wryly: 'I'd like to believe that you meant that, Melissa.'

'I think I do,' she said on a sudden, impulsive surge of affection, and gratitude that he didn't blow hot and cold so that a girl just didn't know where she was with him. 'I felt quite jealous when you and Vicki were getting on so well. I don't think I'd like to lose you now, Neville.'

His arm tightened about her. 'It's possible that you've got me for life,' he said softly and kissed her without a care for watching eyes. 'Could you bear it?'

'Let me think about it just a little longer,' she pleaded, taking sudden fright at the words that were almost a proposal.

But she spent the rest of the evening clinging quite desperately to the comfort of his affection for her, trying not to care that her rejection of Ben's blatantly expressed need had obviously driven him straight into Vicki's delighted arms.

She didn't doubt that his present mood would result in them going to bed together later that night. He would take Vicki just as lightly and as meaninglessly as he had taken her, Melissa thought unhappily. It seemed that any woman would serve in his ruthless pursuit of sexual satisfaction. What a fool she had been to expect any real affection or warmth or tenderness from such a man. She wondered if he was even capable of loving any woman . . . even the one who had let him down. Perhaps his pride had felt the blow much more keenly than his heart.

Fortunately, he wasn't the only man in the world. She

ignored the instinctive and very foolish prompting of her heart which stubbornly insisted that he was as far as she was concerned. Neville could give her everything that Ben Gregory offered—and so much more, she decided proudly. Because he really did love her and might even marry her if she played her cards right. Any girl must be happy with someone as caring and as considerate as her good-looking cousin.

At the end of the evening, the party broke up with Vicki's light-hearted announcement that they were all invited back to Ben's place on the beach for a midnight swim. It was a beautiful night with a full moon and it would be the perfect ending to a perfect day, she declared, with a meaningful glance for the man who stood with his arm wound about her slender waist.

The sudden pain that pierced Melissa's breast was almost unbearable. Her hands clenched so fiercely that the nails dug crescents into the palms. Her eyes locked with Ben's above Vicki's dark head and she didn't care if he recognised the anguish and the longing and the desperate protest in the way she looked at him.

If he really wanted *her* as much as he claimed, how could he even think of making love to Vicki in her stead? How could he smash her lovely memories of that night with him into a million pieces and fill her heart with mourning for the might have been? How could it have meant so little to him that he was able to strike such a cruel blow at hopes and dreams that still survived his blunt declaration that he didn't love her and never would?

'What a lot of faint-hearts!' Vicki jeered as most of the party melted away with a murmur of excuses, mostly

tactful. She turned to Melissa, smiling, serenely unaware of undercurrents. 'How about you and Neville?
You'll come, won't you?'

'Count us out,' Melissa said brightly, slipping her
hand through Neville's arm with that seemingly casual
air of belonging to him that she had deliberately emphasised for Ben's benefit. 'The sea's much too cold at this
time of the year and we've better things to do than invite
pneumonia. Haven't we, darling?' The smile she bestowed on Neville was full of promise.

There hadn't been even a flicker of understanding or
reassurance in Ben's grey eyes and she simply couldn't
go on breaking her heart over such a hard, uncaring
man, she thought proudly. She would do her best to
forget him in Neville's arms that very night.

She managed not to say goodnight to Ben in the flurry
of farewells and car horns and flashing lights in the car
park. Just as she had managed not to speak to him
directly ever since Vicki had persuaded him to join the
group who were celebrating her birthday. Following her
obvious lead, he had virtually ignored her, too.

Vicki got into the white Mercedes as though it was an
old friend and waved gaily to Melissa as it shot off into
the night. One or two cars followed in its wake but there
was a noticeable lack of enthusiasm for Vicki's scheme.
Melissa wondered how many would actually make it to
Spelby and Ben's bungalow and suspected that the
midnight swim would turn into a very intimate affair for
just two people.

As Neville drove the short distance to the flat, slowly
and carefully with an eye to lurking police cars, she
hugged her arms across her hurting breast and stared

unseeingly ahead at the ribbon of road illumined by the car's headlights. She chatted gaily about the success of the evening—silence would be fatal, she felt. She would probably dissolve into the tears that were filling her heart to overflowing.

'Coffee . . . ?' she suggested brightly as the car reached the house.

Neville nodded, turned off the ignition. 'Make it black, love. I've a long way to drive and I guess I've had a lager too many,' he said wryly.

Melissa envied him the slight euphoria of intoxication. She was stone cold sober and it was going to be the hardest thing in the world to open her arms to Neville as she must.

Her heart throbbed and her body was ice as her thoughts revolved constantly about the tormenting image of Vicki, responding to Ben's sensual kisses and the urgent passion that swept aside every consideration but the need for its satisfaction. Vicki, pleasing and delighting him with a response that came from an experience that Melissa lacked, soaring to the heights of her own ecstatic fulfilment in his eager, exciting and very expert embrace. Vicki, falling in love as easily as she always did and perhaps being loved in return. For men *did* love Vicki, much more than she ever loved them. She won hearts so easily, and it could be that Ben did have a heart to lose to the right woman. She just hadn't been that woman. Vicki was her friend and she was fond of her but she couldn't bear to think that she might find a lasting happiness with the one man that Melissa would love and want for the rest of her life, come what may.

She hadn't known that love would fill her being to the

exclusion of everything else and forgive every slight, every hurt, every disappointment and dismay. She hadn't known that it would hurt so much or that she would want to die if she lost Ben to Vicki or anyone else.

She had always been so level-headed, so sure that she could cope with loving when it eventually happened, never doubting that the right man would come along at the right time to round off her well-organised life. Loving a man like Ben was madness, overwhelming her completely, turning her whole world upside down. He just wasn't the right kind of man for a girl like herself. But he was the only man. She would never love anyone else.

Least of all Neville who was so dear and familiar, and would always be more of a brother to her than the lover he longed to be.

As soon as Neville closed the flat door, Melissa moved against him, putting her arms about him, lifting her face to be kissed. There was a kind of desperation in the way that her lips clung and her arms tightened about him.

He held her away, his body responding too quickly to her nearness. 'Oh, darling . . .' He sighed. 'Don't push me too far. I'm only human—and I'm not quite sober,' he warned her.

She smiled into his eyes. 'Then I can't let you drive another twenty miles at this time of night. You'll just have to stay.' She forced the words out, trying to sound matter-of-fact.

He reached to cradle her pretty face in both hands. 'I refuse to sleep on that lumpy sofa,' he protested, a mixture of laughter and pleading in his voice.

'Then you can have the bed.' Her heart was thumping.

'I refuse to let *you* sleep on that lumpy sofa,' he returned promptly, eyes twinkling.

She managed to smile. 'Then we'll share the bed.'

It was so low that he had to strain to catch the words, she knew. But it would never have been easy for Melissa to offer herself in cold blood to any man, with or without love. It had taken Ben Gregory to kindle such a fierce flame of wanting that there hadn't been time or inclination to wonder if it was right or wrong to melt into his arms. Somehow it *had* been right, so natural, the destined coming together of lovers. Even now, she didn't regret the golden glory of that loving. She only regretted that it had meant so little to Ben when it had meant all the world to her.

Neville looked down at her, unsure. He didn't trust her sudden capitulation, she realised. She gave a shaky laugh. 'I don't think you want me after all,' she said, not quite teasing, almost hoping.

'I love you,' he said simply. 'I'm not sure that you love me.'

'Oh, Neville . . .' She touched her lips to his, and kissed him tenderly with a warmth of feeling that she hoped would be more convincing than the lie she couldn't bring herself to utter. His mouth quickened in swift response and he drew her to him with sudden urgency. Melissa tried not to shrink from the meaningful throb of his body's need.

She realised her mistake as soon as he began to make love to her with confident lips and hands. The memories of Ben were too vivid and she found herself comparing every kiss, every caress—to poor Neville's disadvantage.

He couldn't fire her to that tumult of desire. He couldn't kindle even a flicker of that bright flame . . . and Melissa couldn't tell him that he was too patient, too tender, too considerate, that she seemed to need the fierce and demanding and quite ruthless passion of a strongly sensual man who had swept her into instant and overwhelming response. For the first time she really understood the importance of a sexual chemistry between lovers and she knew that any relationship with Neville would be a betrayal, not so much of her love for another man but more of her own instincts and needs. She might love Neville dearly but he wasn't the right man for her and she mustn't marry him even if he decided he wanted it. He deserved so much more than a wife who could only pretend to want him. Such a marriage would be cheating them both.

Neville was much too experienced not to realise the lack of real response in the way she kissed and held him. He was suddenly still, laying his head on her soft breast in defeat. 'It isn't any good, is it?' he asked quietly, heavily. 'You just don't want me at all.'

Melissa stroked the silky blond hair, trying to comfort him. 'I'm sorry . . .' Words were so inadequate, she thought unhappily. What could she say when he was so deeply hurt, so bitterly disappointed and so wounded in his very tender pride? She wondered that he didn't hate her—she had been so encouraging only to disappoint him. But she knew that he loved her—and that made it so much worse.

'So am I.' He rolled away from her to sit on the side of the bed with his head in his hands, struggling with his feelings.

Melissa wanted to cry. For his hurt and for her own. For the unwelcome change in his feelings for her that had ruined the easy and undemanding and very pleasant relationship that as cousins they had always known and enjoyed. And for her inability to take another man in Ben's place, even when there seemed to be no future in keeping herself for him.

'I guess it's the sofa for me, after all,' Neville said wryly. 'Unless you want me to leave . . . ?'

'No . . . of course not!' How could she send him out into the night to drive twenty long miles in his present frame of mind? There was no reason why he shouldn't stay the night and she didn't care if people did talk. He *was* her cousin, after all. 'Oh, Neville! I feel absolutely dreadful,' she sighed, putting her hand out to him impulsively, just as much in need of comfort as he was and scarcely knowing where to look for it now that it wasn't to be found in his arms, in spite of all her efforts.

He turned and took her into his arms and held her, soothing, reassuring. 'There's no need. I do understand, you know,' he said gently, touching his lips to her pale hair.

Melissa doubted it. But it was so like her kind-hearted and sensitive cousin to stifle his own feelings and do what he could to ease her mind and her conscience. She wondered why it was so impossible for her to love him as he deserved—all because of a man who didn't deserve to be loved at all.

'I guess it just isn't the right time—for either of us,' Neville went on slowly, thoughtfully. 'You're wiser than I am. You knew that we shouldn't rush our fences. Tonight you were just wanting to please me. Not wanting me at all. It does take time to adjust, I know. I love you, but I find it hard not to think of you as "little Melissa". Even when I'm making love to you. It's inhibiting. So it's bound to be harder for you when you still aren't sure how you feel about me.'

She put an arm about his neck and laid her cheek against his, hoping to soften the coming blow with the warmth of her very real affection and concern. 'I don't love you, Neville,' she said gently. 'I know I never will . . .' She had to be honest. Truth might hurt but it was not as bad as lying to him or giving him false hope for the future.

Which was exactly what Ben had meant, she suddenly realised. Perhaps he had cared enough to be honest with her in exactly the same way, trying to protect her from building hopes and dreams on a false foundation. Wasn't she trying to guard Neville from further hurt with those blunt, uncompromising words because she cared about him? Maybe Ben had sensed the way she felt about him and known that he must warn her that he had little to give in return. He couldn't be as indifferent as her dismayed heart had instantly assumed—but he *was* proud. Resentment at her refusal to accept that he was prompted by integrity and a genuine concern might have been more instrumental in driving him into Vicki's arms than a need for sexual satisfaction. He might have been taking a very effective revenge.

Neville was silent for a few moments. Then he said quietly, 'This has never happened to me before. It's always been the other way around—me letting the girl down gently. So I know how you feel, Melissa. I won't make it any harder for you. No one can love to order, after all.' He put her away from him resolutely. He rose, buttoning his shirt, reached for his jacket and moved towards the door. 'I've changed my mind about staying. I just can't face that sofa,' he told her wryly.

Melissa wrapped a thin silk robe about herself, belatedly self-conscious about her nudity, and went with him to the door of the flat.

He kissed her for the last time as a lover, his lips sliding briefly across her own. 'I won't see you for a couple of weeks. It won't mean that I'm not thinking about you.'

She put her hand to his cheek in a little gesture of affection. 'I'll miss you,' she said, meaning it.

Watching him walk away from her, her heart was sad that both old and new understandings were lost because he had fallen in love and she hadn't. Melissa knew it might be a very long time before they could get back to their former footing as cousins and friends.

She waited until Neville slid behind the wheel of his low-slung sports car that gleamed in the light of the street lamps and lifted his hand in a final wave. Then, as he drove away, she closed the door with a sigh.

If she had waited for a few more moments she would have seen a familiar white Mercedes with its distinctive number plate passing the house at speed and she would have been prepared for the open antagonism that greeted her when she followed the impulse to visit the bungalow on the beach that Sunday afternoon.

But how could Melissa have known that instead of taking Vicki to Spelby with him that night, Ben had taken her home and left her with a perfunctory kiss before driving back to Chelmer Avenue, haunted by the look in another girl's eyes and his own conviction that no matter what she might say or do, her arms ached to hold him again? Or that he had recognised the silver sports car parked outside the house and waited with a grim expression and growing anger to see how long it remained there, prepared to wait all night if necessary? And that it had only needed her eventual appearance at the door with Neville, wearing only the thin robe that outlined every curve of her slender body, to convince him that she was wanton and unreliable and that he had abruptly lost all desire for her?

After hours of tussling with the level head that told her she was a fool and deserved all the pain and humiliation that was certainly coming her way, Melissa followed the promptings of her tormented heart and set off to see Ben.

She drove to the adjoining village to Spelby, which wasn't quite so popular with the holiday crowds, parked her car and then walked via the cliffs and the beach to the cluster of bungalows that nestled among the dunes.

Heart pounding, a little sickness at the pit of her stomach, not even knowing if she would find him at home on this hot, glorious afternoon, Melissa tried not to rehearse what she would say to him as she made her way towards the wooden little house.

She knew instinctively that it was a scene that could only be played by ear. She had no idea how he would react to her arrival on his doorstep, uninvited, unexpected and maybe unwelcome. But that sudden flash of insight into his possible motives for being so blunt about his strictly dishonourable intentions had given her new hope for the future of their relationship.

He had been honest about his lack of feeling for her. Why shouldn't she be just as honest about the extent of her feeling for him? Loving him wasn't a crime. Loving him, she would try not to make demands on him that he couldn't meet. Loving him, she would try to be content with the little that he could give her as long as they were together. Loving him, she wanted him more than anything in the world and there was no point in pretending that it wasn't so.

She arrived at the bungalow eventually, hot, dusty and thirsty. The door stood wide open to admit the slightest breeze from the sea on the very hot afternoon and Melissa was relieved by that obvious indication of his presence.

She paused at the foot of the wooden steps. She could hear the sound of a radio playing pop music. Wet towels were draped over a line that was slung between the wooden posts of the verandah. He had apparently been for a swim.

Melissa mounted the first step, suddenly so consumed with shyness and excitement and tense apprehension that she had to force herself forward.

'Anyone home . . . ?' she called, horrified to hear the croaking little sound that emerged from her dry throat. 'Ben . . . ?'

He strode to the open door to glower at her, his eyes blazing in a face that had abruptly lost its attractive tan because of the intensity of his anger. 'What are *you* doing here?' he demanded, so coldly that she was frozen where she stood . . .

CHAPTER NINE

THE BLOOD drained from Melissa's face too, leaving it deathly pale. The dark blue eyes flinched from the dislike and contempt in that steely glare. He had hurt her before but it was nothing to the pain that radiated now from the centre of her breast and swept over her in waves, leaving her sick and dizzy and faint.

She groped for the wooden handrail for support. Her eyes were blinded with the tears that all the pride in the world couldn't have kept at bay. She dug her teeth so fiercely into her bottom lip that she tasted blood. It was impossible for her to smile, to speak or even to turn away until she had coped with the shock of all that angry hatred in the way he looked and spoke.

Then she saw Vicki, emerging from what was obviously a bedroom, wearing only the briefest of bikinis, smiling and confident and very lovely.

'Oh!' Melissa didn't recognise the stricken sound as her own voice. 'I didn't know . . . I'm sorry . . .'

'Melissa! What a lovely surprise!' Vicki was genuinely pleased to see her friend. Fiddling with the strap of her bikini top, she didn't notice the hostility in Ben's eyes and manner or the shocked dismay of Melissa's expression. 'Where's Neville?' she demanded lightly, just as though he was always to be found at her friend's side, making matters worse.

'He isn't with me . . . I'm on my own—out for a walk.'

Floundering, Melissa knew she couldn't sound convincing.

'And then you saw Ben?' It was absent, unquestioning. Vicki looked at Melissa fully for the first time and frowned. 'You look as if you've been overdoing it in this heat,' she scolded. 'Come in and sit down and I'll get you something to drink.'

'Yes. It is hot.' Melissa gratefully seized on the excuse that Vicki had provided for the way she was sure that she looked. 'But I won't come in . . . I'm intruding . . .' There was little doubt of that, she knew. Ben was obviously raging, a pulse throbbing in his lean cheek. He didn't add to Vicki's invitation by look or word or attitude.

'Don't be silly!' Vicki laughed at the absurdity. 'Ben, bring her in and make her sit down to rest while I make some tea . . .' She turned to enter the kitchen, blissfully unaware of the anger in the surgeon or the dismay with which Melissa greeted the light words.

She was very much at home in the bungalow and very much at ease with Ben, Melissa observed with pain. How could she doubt that their relationship had progressed rapidly from mere acquaintance to lovers overnight? She didn't blame Vicki. He was a very attractive man and a forceful one and Vicki couldn't have known that she lay in arms that had recently embraced her friend in similar intimacy. And Ben was quite free to love where he wished, of course. Melissa had no claim on him, no right to resent all that had obviously happened since he and Vicki left the dance together on the previous night. But she would never forgive him.

She couldn't look at him as Vicki vanished into the kitchen. And he looked at some spot just above her fair head and said coldly, 'You'd better come in. Make yourself at home.'

'No—I . . .' She shook her head, her words trailing away as she choked on emotion. She turned to hurry from his hostility, his obvious anger at her invasion of his privacy. Her foot slipped on the crumbling wooden step and she was thrown slightly off balance. Ben moved then, to catch her almost roughly by the arm, to steady her. It was instinctive rather than concerned, Melissa knew. 'I'm all right . . .' She shook off his hand, unable to bear his touch.

He looked down at her, stony-faced. 'Why did you come?' he demanded tensely with an anger out of all proportion to the offence.

'I don't know! I thought . . . you said . . .' Melissa's defensive retort broke off abruptly at the sudden, frightening blaze that again leaped in the grey eyes.

'You can forget what I said—and everything else,' he said grimly. 'Wipe it off the slate. It's over—finished! It should never have happened at all.'

'You're telling me!' she flared, her own anger rising rapidly to consume her anguish and bewilderment. She had never lacked spirit and she had her own pride, surfacing at last. 'I must have been quite mad to get involved with someone like you!'

Even in the midst of fury, she wondered what she had done to merit such treatment. Had she struck such a mortal blow at his already wounded pride with her foolish declaration that she had only gone into his arms out of sympathy? He could never have believed such a claim in the light of her warm and willing response to his passion, surely!

Perhaps it had all been very unimportant to him. Perhaps Vicki suited him very much better in every way. But he didn't have to look and sound as though he hated her, Melissa thought, torn between hurt and anger.

'It was a very brief involvement. I think we must both be thankful to put an end to it.' He added deliberately, very harsh, 'I wish it was possible never to see you again.'

'It isn't. We have to work together,' she reminded him coolly. 'I won't like it any more than you will, believe me!'

'If I can do anything about that, then I will,' he promised her savagely.

Vicki carried a tray from the kitchen. 'Ben! Melissa! Tea's ready . . .' She glanced curiously at the couple who seemed so intent on their conversation that they didn't hear her call. She put down the tray and went to join them, sliding her hand through Ben's arm with a casual friendliness that was so characteristic and could be so deceptive. 'I've made tea,' she repeated lightly. 'And I found some biscuits in a cupboard. Not much else, though. What *do* you live on, Ben? Love?' It was bright and teasing and she didn't wait for a reply or notice the faint frown of distaste in the grey eyes. 'Melissa, you're still standing about in this hot sun and you look dreadful!' she declared with the sweeping, brutal frankness of friendship.

Entirely against her will, Melissa was hustled into the cool shade of the bungalow and installed in a chair with a refreshing cup of tea by the briskly determined Vicki, who could make the strongest of men quail and obey when she was on duty on Men's Surgical. It was easier to give in to her well-meaning juggernaut friend than to protest and have to find reasons for protesting, she decided wearily.

Vicki chattered gaily about the dance and teased Melissa about her conquest of Neville, declaring that he was a terrific catch and that she ought to hold on to him with both hands.

Ignoring Melissa, Ben tuned the radio to a cricket commentary and sat on the verandah to listen, with the air of a man who adopted an indulgent attitude to feminine chat but couldn't be expected to pay any attention to it.

Melissa was thankful that Vicki didn't expect more than half an ear and the occasional smiling murmur of agreement. She sat with her back to the bedroom door, dreading to catch even a glimpse of the tumbled bed where they must have been lying in each other's arms before she arrived on the scene. As she'd entered the bungalow, she had seen the chair just inside the door with Vicki's clothes thrown carelessly across it. For a nurse, she was surprisingly untidy off duty.

Pretending to listen, Melissa studied her friend's pretty face and dark curls, her merry brown eyes, the slender, lissom body in the brief bikini, and tried hard to be dispassionate about losing Ben to someone she liked so much. She had always known that Vicki was much more popular with men than herself. She knew just how to handle them, of course. It seemed that she knew exactly how to please and satisfy Ben, too. Melissa thought bleakly that she had probably been too intense, too ready to love, too sensitive about his utter failure to care anything for her in return. Vicki would never make those mistakes.

Now, she was much too light-hearted to care that Melissa knew she had just risen from Ben's bed on a summer afternoon or to mind if a dozen friends turned up to share the rest of the day with her and the surgeon. But he was in no mood for the company of a third person, particularly herself. He must be feeling just a little uncomfortable in the circumstances, Melissa decided. He was certainly angry.

No doubt he thought she took a perverse delight in lingering when she knew that he wanted her to leave. But in fact, she just couldn't yet face the walk along the beach and the cliffs to her parked car, the drive to the empty flat with its too-many reminders and the long, desolate evening ahead with nothing to do but ache for him and grieve for the might have been, and regret that she had sent Neville away with a similar heartache.

Vicki was not as insensitive as she seemed to Ben's silence and his pretended absorption in the cricket or to the haunting misery in Melissa's dark blue eyes. She liked the surgeon but she preferred her men to be less enigmatic and more consistent. Last night, he had been surprisingly attentive only to turn offhand as soon as they drove away from the dance, and she had been astonished when he turned up at her home to whisk her out to lunch and then take her to the beach without a word of warning. It proved the potency of the man's charm—when he chose to exercise it—that she had meekly agreed to his every suggestion, she thought wryly. Now, she wondered if he had been expecting

Melissa that afternoon and deliberately arranged that she shouldn't find him alone. It was really a very puzzling affair. Particularly as Ben hadn't attempted to make even the lightest of love to her.

She decided that it was time to make herself scarce and allow them to sort out their obvious differences.

She rose to gather up the cups and take them out to the kitchen. When she returned, she announced lightly, 'Well, I came to the beach to sunbathe and I mean to have half an hour's snooze in the sun. I'll leave you to talk to Ben. You've had enough sun for one day. You are an idiot to walk all this way on such a hot day. When you're ready to go home, Ben will take you to Charby in his car to save you the walk back. Won't you, sweetie?' She gathered up sunglasses and sun oil, and a blanket that lay across a sofa and headed for the steps, dropping a light kiss on Ben's bronze hair in passing.

Melissa carefully didn't meet his eyes as she looked after Vicki who made her way to a sunny shallow of a nearby sand dune and proceeded to make herself comfortable.

Now was the moment to get up and go, she knew. Ben continued to ignore her in that hurtful and humiliating manner. She looked about the sunlit sitting-room of the bungalow with its cane furniture and chintz cushions and curtains, its linoleum-covered floor and bright paintwork. It was more cheerful and more comfortable than she had expected but still not very suitable surroundings for a man like Ben. It was only a temporary home, of course. She wondered if he was still looking for a house in the district and if he would live in it alone or if it would turn out that Vicki shared it with him. There was a heart-wrenching confidence in her friend's easy rapport with the surgeon.

She looked again at her friend, prone and glistening with sun oil, looking at peace with the world and herself. She envied Vicki's ability to fall in love without ever really losing her heart. She could enjoy an affair and then accept it was over without any regret or dismay. She would never feel as lonely and lost and unhappy as Melissa did.

Ben switched off the radio abruptly and got to his feet, his tall and powerful frame blocking the doorway. His grey eyes regarded her intently.

She got up from her chair. 'I'm just going . . .' He said nothing. 'I shouldn't have come here,' she added quietly, wondering why she hesitated to hurl reproach and abuse at that handsome head when he hadn't hesitated to hurt and humiliate her.

'No,' he agreed, very cold. 'You didn't like what you found, I'm afraid.'

Melissa flushed. 'Vicki's a lovely girl,' she said slowly, carefully. 'I'm not blaming you . . .'

'Yes, you are,' he told her bluntly, very brusque. 'You're as jealous as hell. Do you think I don't know just why you came, Melissa?'

'Don't say any more,' she said quickly, with pride, her heart dreading what he might say and her level head suspecting exactly what was in his mind.

She moved towards the door. He blocked her path quite deliberately and shoved the door with a strong hand so that it didn't quite shut but hid them from any curious eyes.

Melissa looked up at him with sudden alarm and

apprehension tingling in her veins. There was a very dangerous glint in those grey eyes that was much more than anger.

'You look so cool, Melissa. So innocent and unaware. You really had me fooled,' he said dryly. 'But you just can't get enough, can you?'

Having not the slightest doubt of what he meant by those sardonic and contemptuous words, Melissa hit him, hard. It was an instinctive, shocked reaction to the insult.

Ben caught her wrist, eyes blazing, gripping her flesh with cruel fingers. He held her captive with an arm behind her back, her slight body thrust willy-nilly against him, while he kissed her with a savage passion that bruised her heart much more than her soft, reluctant mouth.

She caught her breath on a sob that was half anger, half pain, and tried to hit him again with her free hand. He captured that, too. Before she knew what he was about, he had propelled her across the room and into the bedroom. He kicked the door shut and threw her down on the bed.

Melissa instantly struggled to her feet, startled and furious but still not believing what she saw in his eyes.

With both hands on her shoulders, he forced her back on the pillows and held her while he kissed her again with rather more passion than anger this time. She kicked out at him and he came down on her slight body with his own, stifling resistance with his weight.

His kiss became more demanding, his body grew urgent and Melissa tried to throw him off in some little panic, tried to thrust away the hand that crushed the soft flesh of her breast in an almost brutal caress. 'For God's sake, Ben . . . !' She was still more angry than frightened. 'Will you stop it! Do you want me to hate you?'

He caught her chin in his strong hand, forced her to look at him squarely. 'This is what you wanted. Isn't it? This is why you came here. Isn't it? Will you be honest with me—and yourself?'

'I wanted to talk to you!' she exclaimed desperately.

'Rubbish! You want me just as much as I want you! Why the hell couldn't you admit it last night!' He was busy with the buttons of her linen frock, the clip of her bra, ignoring the protest of her hands and body.

'You're mad!' she said in sudden fright as she realised the power and the unrelenting intent of his passion. She broke free, briefly. He dragged her back and pinioned her with his body. 'That's enough, Ben! If you don't stop . . . !'

'What will you do? Cry rape?' He laughed softly and stifled any further protest with his warm, sensual mouth on her own.

Melissa couldn't fight him. He was much too powerful and much too determined. She couldn't yield, either. She resisted him with the rigidity of her slender body, the coldness of her lips and the anger and dismay in her heart.

There was no pleasure for either of them in the silent, stormy union of their bodies. Having lost his temper so completely, he had lost control of that angry tide of passion, too. It was very quickly spent.

Melissa felt numb.

She just couldn't believe that it had happened.

She didn't know what to do or say.

But she knew that he felt very much worse than she did. She was sick, shocked and shaken. Ben was absolutely shattered.

It hurt all the more because she loved him so much. Even now. Even though he had taken her without love or tenderness or even liking to punish her for something that she didn't even know that she had done, she thought heavily.

She ached to hold him to her, to touch her hand to the thick bronze hair that she loved. Sternly, she resisted the impulse and kept hands and arms rigidly at a distance. He didn't deserve to be loved and comforted and forgiven. He had behaved abominably. No wonder he was too ashamed to look at her or even to speak to her—so he should be!

Melissa was desperately afraid and sick at heart. Loving him, there was no hope at all of any happiness with him now. There had been little enough before. Now, he would hate her for what had happened. It would be an instinctive male reaction, an involuntary revulsion of feeling for a woman he had taken against her will in a tumult of rage and desire that had swept him beyond control.

'Let me dress . . .' It came out with hate and loathing and she saw that he flinched from the chill in her stony voice.

He lay very still, face buried in the pillow and an arm flung across his head, while she scrambled into clothes that had surprisingly survived his impatient hands.

'Get up,' she said quietly. 'If Vicki walks in, she'll know immediately what's happened. I think you've humiliated me enough.'

He rolled over to look at her and she saw that the words had struck home. 'I'm sorry you feel like that,' he said levelly, very low.

'How do you expect me to feel?' It was carefully controlled hurt. She knew that it sounded like anger.

'Do you want me to tell you how *I* feel?'

Melissa shook her head. As if she needed to be told that he was filled with remorse and self-loathing and a fierce regret that their relationship was ruined beyond all repair!

Ben reached out to take her hand as if there might yet be some kind of understanding between them. She backed away from him swiftly. 'Don't touch me!' It was a warning rather than the revulsion that he instantly supposed. She didn't think she could bear any more. The look in his eyes was tearing at her heart.

She walked through to the sitting-room, leaving him. Looking through the window, she was relieved to see that Vicki was still lying in the sun, eyes closed and unsuspecting.

Melissa was trembling and her legs were jelly, that dreadful pain was clutching at her heart as if it would never let go again. She wanted to cry but she didn't dare because once started, she might never stop.

Ben came into the room behind her, running his hands through his hair. 'I don't know what to say to you,' he said quietly. 'There ought to be something but I don't know the right words.'

She turned to look at him, head high. 'It will be a long time before you can say anything that I'll want to hear. If ever.' She spoke without heat and it was all the more convincing.

'Then I'll say nothing for the time being.'

'I think that's wise.' Melissa marvelled at her coolness, her composure, when she was falling apart inside. A Hartlake training did wonders for a girl, she thought dryly, preparing her for all eventualities.

She picked up her bag, still lying where she had left it, and moved to the door.

'Let me drive you to Charby . . .'

'No!' She needed to get away from him. She needed time to think and to cope with the way she felt, to prepare herself for the next time that she had to face this man. It didn't help to realise that they would be working together the very next morning.

Monday was always a busy day in Theatres, dealing with the new intake of patients admitted for major surgery. She was his theatre nurse and he was a demanding perfectionist of a surgeon who would expect her very best in any circumstances.

But how would she be able to concentrate on the day's work when she would be reminded at every turn that the man who was so intent on saving and preserving life had ruthlessly destroyed something as precious as a woman's pride and dignity by disregarding her right to say no?

'It's the least I can do. Vicki's right. It's too far for you to walk in this heat . . .'

He was trying to make amends, she realised. As if he could! 'Just leave me alone,' she said tensely with a little choke in her voice. Concern was rather out of place at this moment in time, she thought, engulfed by bitterness.

Ben looked down at her. 'Don't cry!' It was abrupt, harsh. 'I don't think I could stand that . . .'

Her chin went up instantly. 'Don't be so absurd! It would take a better man than you to reduce *me* to tears!' she said proudly.

His mouth twisted in that sardonic, self-mocking, humourless smile. 'It shouldn't be difficult to find one.'

'And I know just where to look,' Melissa declared coldly, striking to hurt even while she wondered why she even supposed that he cared.

She almost ran along the beach towards Charby, carefully by-passing the dune where Vicki lay and carefully not looking back.

Afterwards, she didn't remember a thing about that brisk walk along the beach and the cliffs to her parked car.

But every moment of that angry, determined love-making was indelibly etched on her mind.

She supposed she should hate him. She supposed she should feel that he had committed an unforgivable crime. But she was a very honest girl and she knew that even in the midst of anger and outrage, her body had welcomed his need of her and her heart had been eager to make allowances because she loved him. It was only her shocked mind that had protested with such passionate indignation because he took her against her will.

He had been ruthless rather than violent, he hadn't hurt her at all, she admitted. Maybe because her resistance had been passive rather than active. She had submitted rather than struggle with an angry and powerful man.

In retrospect, she was more puzzled than hurt because of all that anger, directed against her without explanation.

The hurt lay in the knowledge that there hadn't been an atom of love in that lovemaking, and in the contempt of his attitude towards a girl he obviously regarded as 'easy' because it had only needed one kiss, one touch, and she had melted . . .

CHAPTER TEN

As USUAL, Melissa had been busy with a variety of routine tasks for some time before she began to look for some sign of Ben's arrival in Theatres. There was always a heavy list on Mondays and she came on duty early to organise the preparation of the theatre that was her particular responsibility.

There was much to be done. Melissa was glad to be busy as she instructed her junior nurses in the laying-up of trolleys and checked equipment and ran through procedures and made routine calls to the Path Lab and the blood bank. She took pride in always having things ready by the time the surgeon arrived to start work on the day's list.

She didn't feel angry with Ben. She had slept surprisingly well and woken with the quiet, level-headed resolution to behave as though that incident in his bungalow had never happened. Only herself and Ben knew about it, fortunately. Only herself and Ben could handle it so that something was salvaged from the debris of their relationship.

Melissa wasn't at all sure where they went from here. It was up to Ben. Either he wanted no more to do with her—ever; or he felt that they could try again to build some kind of future on a new foundation. Whatever happened, too much had been said and done to be easily forgotten.

Loving him, she didn't mean to punish Ben with a show of hostility and resentment, when she knew instinctively that he bitterly regretted what had happened. Even more than she did.

But she didn't mean to be warm and friendly and forgiving, either. Not just yet. That would only convince him that she regarded that near-rape as an easily forgettable incident in the life of a girl who'd known lots of men. It still bothered her that he probably didn't know she had been a virgin when he stormed into her life and took possession of her on that whirlwind of passion. She suspected that he imagined Neville to be a lover rather than a friend. She wasn't sure if he knew that they were also cousins.

She decided that she must continue to be the efficient theatre nurse who had pleased and impressed him in those first weeks. She wouldn't give him the least cause to complain or to criticise her work or her attitude. She knew just how remote and detached he could be and she was prepared for him to behave as if she was a robot without name or face or identity, who could be trusted to hand the right instrument at the right moment and to anticipate his every need during surgery.

Melissa wondered if working together in the aseptic and unhurried atmosphere of an operating theatre might be the only way that they could both cope with a personal involvement that had got out of control. It was impossible for surgeon and nurse not to share a kind of rapport in the theatre. Somehow the weight of mutual responsibility for a patient's well-being could reduce one's own problems to mere trifles and put one's own feelings into proper perspective.

Just now, she and Ben were as far apart as they could possibly be. They had been strangers, turned suddenly and much too soon into lovers. Now they were strangers again. Given time, they might yet be friends . . .

There was a sudden flurry of activity in Theatres with the news of an admission to Accident and Emergency of a man badly injured in a road accident.

Theatre Sister Cheryl Sherwood sent an urgent message to warn Melissa to prepare for an emergency splenectomy and thoracotomy and advise her that the first patient on that morning's list would be kept in the ward for the time being. Mr Gregory was on his way to scrub-up.

Melissa and her team of nurses bustled about, preparing the equipment that would be required for the removal of a damaged spleen and the repair of a crushed rib cage, probably due to impact with a steering wheel. No doubt the patient had suffered other injuries too, and an efficient theatre nurse kept that in mind and prepared accordingly.

She went to ask Cheryl for the key to the drugs cupboard, needing a further supply of ampoules and hypodermic needles. As she reached the open office door, she paused at the sound of Ben's deep voice, and her heart lurched so violently that it was a moment or two before the tense and apparently angry words actually registered.

'Get her out of that theatre as soon as possible! She won't be assisting me!'

'But what can I say to her? She *is* your theatre nurse and she's expecting to assist!'

Cheryl sounded unusually flustered. Ben had a talent

for upsetting people with the brusqueness of his manner.
He was being particularly brusque this morning, Melissa
thought, in an oddly detached fashion.

'I don't care how you do it but get her out of that
theatre now and give me another nurse—and keep
Nurse Warren busy elsewhere!'

'I suppose I must . . .'

'Yes, you must!'

'It won't be easy . . .'

'You're wasting time, Sister!'

Melissa didn't wait to hear more. She turned away
blindly and went back to the theatre. She automatically
checked the trolley that a nurse presented for her inspec-
tion and refused to think or feel anything else until her
shocked mind and heart could accept what he had done.

How he must hate her. How he must despise her. He
knew that she was a good theatre nurse, efficient and
reliable and responsible, invaluable in an emergency as
she had already proved on several occasions. How *could*
he allow his personal feelings to colour his attitude to his
work and his duty to his patients?

Anger began to take the place of shock and dismay.
How dared he refuse to work with her and insist that she
was replaced before he would set foot in the theatre to
deal with his patient? St Biddulph's would be buzzing
with the humiliation that he inflicted on her with such
behaviour. She had forgiven him everything else. She
would never, never forgive him this!

Cheryl appeared in the doorway, flushed and looking
harassed, just a few minutes before the emergency was
due to arrive in Theatres. 'Oh, Nurse Warren! I want
you, please!'

The formality of tone and manner and address was a very clear indication that she disliked the surgeon's insistence on her removal from the theatre but felt she had to humour him, Melissa thought bleakly. She responded with well-trained obedience, immediately leaving what she was doing.

'Yes, Sister?'

'Is everything quite ready for Mr Gregory's patient?'

'Yes, Sister. He should be here at any moment and I believe that Mr Gregory has arrived,' she said carefully.

'Yes. He's getting ready to scrub up. Now, I know it's very short notice,' she went on hastily, 'but I want you to change theatres and assist Mr Savage this morning. He has a very tricky ovariectomy on his list and you've had a lot of experience in gynae surgery at Hartlake, haven't you?'

The plump and jolly and usually hard to ruffle Theatre Sister seemed rushed and ill at ease and didn't quite meet Melissa's eyes as she spoke. Melissa thought bitterly that she knew why. Cheryl was embarrassed and sorry for her and she didn't want it to show. Ben Gregory had put her in a quite impossible position.

She wondered why someone whose word was law in Theatres for all her easy good nature should have allowed the surgeon to dictate to her on such a matter. He was compelling and forceful, she knew, but he really had no right to insist that any particular nurse should or should not work with him. She was surprised that Cheryl hadn't promptly told him so and refused to move her staff around to suit his whims.

'But this is my theatre, Sister. And I always work with Mr Gregory,' she pointed out with dry lips and thudding heart, knowing that she would be expected to make some protest. And she was too proud not to protest, deeply hurt, bitterly humiliated and near to hating a man who knew just how to take his revenge on a nurse who loved her work and knew it to be good.

'Yes, I know. But I want you to work with Mr Savage today, please,' Cheryl said firmly. 'Nurse Hastings has already been told to take over from you. Now come along, Nurse. There's a lot to do before that ovariectomy comes up and it isn't like you to argue . . .'

She was obviously anxious to hustle her from the theatre before Ben arrived, as instructed.

'Very well, Sister.' It was reluctant but Melissa was too well trained to question the dictums of a senior or to refuse to obey without very good cause.

She cast a last proprietorial eye over the prepared theatre, gleaming and sterile and perfectly in order, and left in Cheryl's hurrying wake just as the lift gave a familiar little whine and its doors opened to reveal a tableau of the emergency trolley with its unconscious patient surrounded by the hovering medical team from A and E.

Melissa's glance was fleeting and professional and she only caught a glimpse of the patient before he was wheeled out of the lift and along to the theatre.

Ben came out of the surgeons' changing-room, wearing green tunic and trousers, on his way to scrub up while the anaesthetist prepared the patient for surgery.

Melissa had to pass him but she didn't have to speak. Their eyes met. She looked at him with loathing and wasn't surprised that he didn't make the slightest move to speak or smile. The grey eyes looked back at her without expression and she hurried on. She sensed that he looked after her and she stiffened her back with pride and fury . . .

John Savage was a delightful man, some of the bedside manner that his gynaecological patients loved rubbing off on the theatre staff. He was pleasant and courteous and appreciative, a slow and fussy surgeon with smiling eyes above the green mask and warm humour in the soft voice as he joked with the nurses over the recumbent patient.

Melissa should have enjoyed the leisurely atmosphere of working with him that morning and been relieved that she didn't have to stifle her feelings and endure mutual hostility in order to assist Ben as usual. But she missed the swift sureness of Ben's skilled hand with knife and needle, the caustic tongue that kept everyone on their toes, the attitude that not only expected but demanded that everyone should give of their best. As *he* did.

Assisting Ben was a challenge that she always liked to feel she could meet, Melissa realised. She felt that she owed it to her Hartlake training and to her own confidence in her ability to satisfy the perfectionist trait in a dedicated and demanding surgeon.

John Savage had finished his list and left before the accident victim was transferred to the intensive care unit with a more optimistic prognosis than when he had arrived in Theatres. There had been considerable internal haemorrhaging as well as the ruptured spleen, and a punctured lung from the crushed rib cage. It had taken over three hours to deal with the delicate and intricate task of operating to repair the damage and save the man's life.

Busy in the other theatre, Melissa had known very little of what was going on but she didn't doubt that Ben was doing his best. She was in the clinical room, preparing instruments for the autoclave at the end of the morning's work with John Savage, when he walked in.

She didn't look at him and she didn't speak. She had nothing to say to him. She went on with her work.

Ben leaned against the door, silent.

Melissa glanced at him, very briefly. He was still wearing surgical greens but he had taken off the theatre gown and mask. She saw that he was tired. He was pinching the bridge of his nose to ease the slight strain of intense concentration beneath bright arc lights that took its eventual toll on a surgeon's eyes.

She knew that he was waiting for her to turn to him, to say something to him. She would not, she determined. She had made the mistake of showing friendship too many times. She had given far too much too willingly— and for what? Insult and humiliation and an assault that was best forgotten.

She kept her back carefully turned and the silence became heavy with his tension and her stubborn hostility.

He erupted with sudden savagery. 'Damn you! Will you look at me! I've strained every bloody nerve to keep that man alive for your benefit and the least you can do is turn round and talk to me!'

Melissa had turned, quite involuntarily, startled into dropping an instrument at the same time. It lay unheeded on the floor as she stared at him, shocked by his tone and puzzled by the words.

'What *are* you talking about? What man? I don't know what you . . . *oh*!' Seeing that he instantly regretted his angry and revealing words, realising just what she was reading in the grey eyes that met her own with sudden compassion in their depths, Melissa's heart plunged with alarm. 'Do you mean *Neville* . . . ? That emergency . . . !' She put a hand to the table to steady herself as shock sent the blood draining from her face and coursing icily through her veins. '*Neville!*'

'His car went off the road. It's bad but he'll do,' he said brusquely.

He sounded indifferent. But he was too good a surgeon not to be deeply concerned for his patient, she knew. Too caring a man, she admitted fairly. Melissa, even in her dismay and disbelief, found herself wondering if he used the hospital terminology for a patient expected to make a full recovery because he really believed it or to comfort her.

She tried to marshall her thoughts and emotions, fighting panic and pain. She tried to acquaint that brief glimpse of a near-to-death patient being rushed into Theatres with Neville, the dear and familiar and much-loved cousin that she had so recently sent away disappointed.

'Neville . . .' she repeated blankly.

Now, suddenly, everything was falling into place.

Those curt, overheard words that now took on a very different meaning. Cheryl's anxiety to hurry her from the theatre and the warm sympathy that she had sensed and misunderstood. The decision to keep her fully occu-

pied in another theatre while Ben operated on the badly
hurt Neville. The vague feeling during the morning that
there was a conspiracy among her colleagues to avoid all
mention of the emergency that was taking so much of the
time and skill of the SSO in the adjoining theatre.

She had decided that she was being too sensitive and
that whatever explanation Ben had given Cheryl for
refusing to work with her that morning would not have
been passed on by the kindly, warm-hearted Theatre
Sister.

Now she realised that they had all been well-meaning
efforts to protect her from the truth until Ben could
bring her better news of Neville's condition.

'So *that's* why you wouldn't let me assist!' He had been
thinking of her feelings rather than his own, after all. She
was sorry that she had misjudged him so badly. But she
was still indignant.

'You're fond of him.'

It was very typical understatement, she realised. But
this was not the moment to put him right on the degree of
her affection for Neville.

'Of course I'm fond of him! But did you really think
that I'd go completely to pieces!' she demanded angrily.

He shrugged. 'It was a chance that I couldn't afford to
take. You know that.'

Melissa did know. But she wasn't prepared to accept
that the shock of seeing her cousin wheeled unexpectedly into the theatre for surgery would reduce a highly-
trained and very efficient Hartlake nurse to an emotional and incompetent wreck that was of no use in such an
emergency. She felt that she had been cheated of the

right to do what she had been trained to do in order to help the cousin she loved.

'Why wasn't I *told*?'

Ben hesitated. 'That was my decision,' he admitted. 'Perhaps it was too hastily made. But I thought it was the right thing at the time.'

'When did you ever do *anything* right as far as I'm concerned?' Melissa threw at him, most unfairly. She didn't care that his eyes hardened and narrowed as though the words had hit home. 'You know nothing about me! How *could* you say nothing and bundle me out of the way while Neville . . . while he . . .' She broke off abruptly and covered her eyes with a shaking hand, fighting the emotion that he had obviously dreaded inviting into the operating theatre.

Ben was silent.

How could Melissa know that he was longing to hold her and comfort and reassure her and that he was effectively checked by the way that she had looked at him earlier and the way she spoke to him now? With contempt and loathing. With an utter lack of the forgiveness that he had foolishly expected from a sweet-natured and warmly generous girl who had never deserved the way he had treated her.

Or this last cruel blow. Well, he had done his best for the man who apparently meant so much to her. Now, all that remained was to keep out of her life in the future and stifle that persistent conviction that he had learned to love deeply for the first time in his life.

Only a week ago, he had scarcely been aware of her as anything but an efficient theatre nurse who had a gift for blending into the background when she wasn't actively engaged in assisting him during surgery. Now, it shook him considerably to discover how important she had become to him.

His feeling for Delia had rapidly receded into the distance ever since he had admitted his desire for this pretty, spirited and enchanting girl. The need that she had inspired was turning out to be much more than merely physical, he thought ruefully.

Melissa pulled herself together. Tears were a weakness that only belonged to the minor blows in life. Like losing her very foolish heart to a man who would never want it and having all her hopes and dreams of happiness with him shattered in one fell blow.

Real tragedy went too deep for tears, she knew. Hadn't she coped with losing both her parents in that sailing disaster and never once broken down? She had never ceased to grieve for them but no one had ever seen her cry.

Nurses are so hard, someone had once said in her hearing, critical. Melissa had been instantly incensed. Nurses learn the hard way to hide their feelings, she had wanted to exclaim in swift and angry defence. They have to grow an extra skin at an early stage of their training or give up nursing.

Nurses see so many tragedies and their effects, and they have to suppress their own feelings and get on with the business of comforting patients and relatives, helping them come to terms with those tragedies. There was no time in a busy hospital for wasteful or unhelpful sentiment and a brisk, practical approach might seem cold and callous but rallied many a patient out of dangerous self-pity or lethargy, and prodded them on the way to recovery.

'He's in the IC Unit, I suppose? I want to see him,' she said firmly.

Ben nodded. 'Of course.'

'How is he . . . *really*?'

He told her, pulling no punches.

Melissa listened carefully. Knowing the worst, she could begin to hope for the best. Neville might be seriously ill but he was alive. He was very fit, very resilient, and he had a buoyancy of spirit that would surely carry him through this difficult time in his life. It might be a long job but he would be well again. In the meantime, he would need her—and she knew that she must be there for him. Nothing else really mattered just now, she felt.

'What about the family? They know, I suppose? Are any of them here? Parents . . . sisters?'

'His parents. I'm on my way to see them right now, in fact.'

'I'd better come with you. They'll expect to see me. They must wonder why I haven't already told them what's happening to Neville and how he is.'

'I believe they asked for you and were told that you were still on duty.' He looked down at her with slight concern. 'Are you up to seeing them? Mrs Page is very distressed, I gather.'

'I must. She doesn't trust doctors but she'll believe me if I tell her that Neville's going to be fine. As he is!' Melissa said firmly.

'Everything is in his favour, certainly,' Ben agreed.

Including a girl like this one, willing and waiting for him to get well, he thought wryly.

They were the only occupants of the lift as it took them to the third floor where the intensive care unit was situated. Standing close to him for once she wasn't conscious of his nearness, his dearness, the physical magnetism that emanated from the tall and too-attractive surgeon who had wrought such havoc in her life. All her thoughts and emotions were tied up with Neville for the time being. Neville loved her and he was hovering in that dreadful limbo between life and death, needing her affection and support and all her prayers.

She doubted if Ben needed her at all. It had probably been a very foolish readiness of her heart and body and usually level head to believe that he did.

When he spoke, she looked at him as though he was a stranger, startled out of her reverie.

'I don't suppose this is the right moment,' he said quietly. 'But I want you to know how much I regret . . . everything.'

Melissa knew what he meant and she knew he was sincere. But it *wasn't* the right moment and she was impatient with him for choosing it.

'We all make mistakes,' she said levelly, non-commital.

His eyes narrowed. 'Was it *all* a mistake, Melissa?'

She heard the rather rueful challenge of the words and chose to ignore it. It probably didn't mean anything, anyway.

He had hurt her so much. Why should she hesitate to hurt him just a little in return?

'From beginning to end, don't you think?' she returned coolly, and stepped out of the lift . . .

CHAPTER ELEVEN

DONNING sterile gown and mask, Melissa was allowed a few moments with Neville, who was on a life support machine following the lengthy surgery, and not yet round from the effects of the anaesthetic.

It tore at her heart to see the golden lad, the darling of the gods, the light-hearted charmer that she dearly loved lying in a hospital bed surrounded by drips and tubes and sophisticated monitoring equipment.

Briefly, she talked to the team who were looking after him. Everyone seemed to know that Neville was important to her. Few seemed to know that he was in fact her cousin. The grapevine wasn't so very efficient, after all, she thought dryly.

Before she left, she went back to the side of Neville's bed. She said his name softly, with love. She touched the hand that had held her own, stroked her hair, caressed her in an urgent desire that hadn't evoked the slightest echo in her own body.

She stooped to kiss him through the mask, touching her lips to the ashen cheek with its faint glimmer of golden stubble, wishing that she was able to love him as he wanted and deserved, and that she hadn't given her heart so impulsively and so irrevocably to a very different kind of man.

Turning away with tears in her eyes, she realised that Ben was watching her through the observation window.

There was an enigmatic expression in his eyes, a grimness about the set of his mouth and an unmistakable tension in that tall, powerful frame.

Her heart trembled. She loved him so much. Why wasn't it possible to run into those strong arms and feel them surround her with love and reassuring support instead of the leaping desire that had been her downfall? Why couldn't he love her as Neville did, for so many other reasons than the sexual delight she could give him?

She went into the ante-room and took off the gown and mask, dropping them in the 'dirty' bin, steeling herself for the task of convincing her aunt and uncle that they had no need to be unduly anxious about Neville.

Ben met her in the corridor and fell into step beside her as she walked towards the waiting-room. 'It seems that I do have to be jealous of Neville,' he said abruptly and without preliminary, reminding her of an assurance that she had impulsively given him on another occasion.

Melissa turned to look at him with a slight challenge in the dark blue eyes. 'I thought you said that jealousy was too strong a word.' Her tone was dry, slightly tart. Her recollection of that conversation with him was just as good as his own, it implied.

'I've decided that it isn't.'

Her heart didn't respond to the implication of the quiet words. Perhaps it no longer dared to hope and dream where he was concerned. Perhaps it just didn't trust anything he said or did any more. Or perhaps it was too full of Neville at that moment to care if another man wanted her enough that he could resent her obvious affection and concern for him.

She looked away from the disturbing glow in the grey

eyes. 'Neville has much more reason to be jealous of you,' she said coolly and turned away to open the door of the waiting-room.

Thoughtfully, he allowed her a few moments alone with Neville's parents before he came into the room to talk to them.

Melissa was very cheerful and brightly optimistic for their sake. She kissed them both and comforted them with the assurance that Neville's condition was stable and satisfactory, that he had the best possible nursing care and every attention and that there was no reason why he shouldn't make an excellent recovery.

They both clung to the thought that she would be on hand to look after him and neither of them seemed able to grasp that she hadn't actually abandoned her job in Theatres to nurse Neville. She didn't pursue the point as it seemed to make them happy to believe it.

They were both being very brave. Neville was their only son, their pride and joy. Melissa still had an arm about her moist-eyed aunt when Ben entered.

'Now, this is Mr Gregory, Aunt Eleanor,' she said gently. 'He's the surgeon who operated on Neville and he's come to tell you how he is now. He's very easy to talk to so don't be afraid to ask anything you want.'

She saw that Ben's eyes narrowed in surprise at the affectionate term of address and the quite unmistakable resemblance between herself and the older woman that she was comforting. It was obviously his first inkling of her relationship to Neville and his parents. She strongly resembled her aunt who had been her mother's twin sister. Neville had inherited his mother's colouring and his father's looks so the likeness between cousins was not so marked.

Ben didn't comment. He sat down and began to explain Neville's extensive injuries and what had been done for him and how long it would probably take to get him back on his feet in a calm, quiet way that soothed the natural fears and anxieties of his parents.

Melissa had never seen him on the wards with his patients and their relatives, or taking his regular clinic in Outpatients. On duty, she only knew him as the impersonal, uncommunicative, hard-working and very demanding surgeon who got on with the job and had no time to waste on personalities or frivolities. Now she saw another side to him. She discovered that he knew exactly the right approach and wasn't at all the arrogant, autocratic and aloof senior doctor who disliked questions and resented any implication of doubt of his ability or experience or prognosis.

She heard the compassion in his voice as he talked to her tearful aunt and saw the patient understanding in his grey eyes as he answered the questions thrown at him in rather militant fashion by her very anxious uncle. He was warmly reassuring and very kind. He was thoughtful and caring and concerned.

There was much more to Ben Gregory than she had known when she toppled headlong into love with him, Melissa admitted. Her heart had recognised the strength and integrity and warmth behind the cool, often austere, always reserved mask that he showed to the world. Her body had responded quite instinctively to the sensuality and passion and need in the tall and powerful and very attractive man. Now, her level head was discovering that there could be many more reasons for loving.

Allowed to look at their son through the observation window of the intensive care unit, her aunt and uncle were then persuaded to go home and return later in the day when Neville would hopefully have regained consciousness.

Having reassured them all over again and waved them off from the hospital car park, Melissa decided it was time for a belated lunch.

But she was scarcely able to eat anything for the unspoken sympathy that she sensed on all sides, the well-meaning smiles and glances and murmurs of comfort from her friends who paused briefly at her table on their way in or out of the nurses' dining-room. It seemed that the ever-efficient grapevine had spread the news that her boyfriend was in the IC Unit and everyone was sorry for her.

She had never realised that she was so well-liked at St Biddulph's or that her affairs—or lack of them—were of so much interest to her fellow nurses. She could only be thankful that no one knew anything about her brief and intimate relationship with the SSO. Life wouldn't be worth living, she thought wryly.

The grapevine had her virtually engaged to Neville, she discovered. It all added to the drama, of course, and it didn't really matter. She might be much happier if she *was* engaged to Neville, even with him lying at death's door, rather than hopelessly in love with someone as unpredictable as Ben Gregory.

She just didn't know what to make of Ben. Thoughtfully trying to protect her from shock and distress by keeping her in ignorance of Neville's condition until he had succeeded in his efforts to improve it through surgery—and then hurling the news at her head with sudden, savage irritation because she went on being busy instead of greeting him when he entered the clinical room. Declaring at one stage that he'd had enough of love and treating her with every appearance of indifference and contempt, using her for his sexual satisfaction with utter disregard for her feelings—and then deciding to be jealous of her affection for Neville and telling her so, just as if he had a right to her love and meant to claim it.

She loved him but she couldn't trust him not to hurt and humiliate her all over again, she decided ruefully. She didn't mean to relent, to weaken, to let him into her arms again until she was really sure that his wanting and his need was based on something more than physical attraction. That day might never dawn, she admitted. In which case, she would either marry a man who did love her as every woman longed and needed to be loved—or settle for the satisfaction and fulfilment that she had always found in nursing.

Seeing her from the servery, Vicki brought her tray over to Melissa's table and sat down with her. 'How's Neville?' she asked immediately.

'He's going to be all right, it seems.' Melissa mustered a smile for her friend in response to that warm and genuine concern.

'What a terrible thing to happen! Poor Neville. Poor you!' Vicki laid a hand briefly on her arm in sympathy. 'Ben was working on him for hours, I gather. Resuscitated him twice.'

Melissa was startled, shocked. Ben hadn't told her

that part. 'Then it's been a very near thing,' she said slowly.

'Heavens yes! He was brought into A and E more dead than alive . . . oh, my wretched tongue!' she exclaimed in instant remorse. 'I am sorry.' She had seen Melissa wince at the words.

'It doesn't matter. I am a nurse. Remember?' Melissa tried to speak lightly.

'Then you know that miracles can and do happen,' Vicki returned promptly. 'And Neville's particular miracle was having a surgeon like Ben Gregory on hand to bring him through. He's really good, isn't he? Julie Hastings has been raving about his technique and his skill and his courage and his refusal to admit defeat. I'm glad you didn't assist.'

'I was banished to assist John Savage with his gynae list.'

'And a good thing, too,' Vicki approved. 'No one should see their nearest and dearest on an operating table.'

'In fact, I didn't know anything about it until it was all over,' Melissa said wryly.

'That was thoughtful of someone.'

'Ben . . .' Melissa hesitated. 'He can be thoughtful,' she added quietly. As well as ruthless and bloody-minded and quite impossible when he wished, she thought ruefully. She loved him just the same.

'I can't make head or tail of the man,' Vicki declared, settling down to enjoy her meal now that the necessary preliminaries had been exchanged.

Melissa raised an eyebrow. 'I thought you liked him,' she said levelly. 'You seemed to be the best of friends.'

She was careful to keep all hint of jealousy or resentment, or even curiosity, from her tone.

'Oh, I *like* him! I'm just grateful that I don't like him too much.' Vicki leaned forward and dropped her voice. 'Strictly in confidence, he's a disappointment, Melissa. A complete waste of a woman's time. He was obviously born to be the kind of bachelor surgeon who breaks every hopeful nurse's heart. He *isn't* engaged, by the way. I shouldn't think he's the type to marry at all, frankly.'

'Then I guess the grapevine got it wrong again,' Melissa said lightly. It seemed that Ben hadn't told Vicki about the girl in Bury St Edmunds that he had hoped to marry and lost to his friend. She didn't know very much about the affair herself, she thought wryly. Either he couldn't bring himself to talk about the woman he loved or he was too sensitive to her own feeling for him and wouldn't hurt her by dwelling on all that he had lost. She smiled at Vicki, rather puzzled by her assertions. 'How is he so disappointing?'

'Not much of a man,' Vicki said bluntly, and with unmistakable meaning. 'Strange, isn't it? He looks so sexy and seems so exciting yet he hasn't got an ounce of real passion in him! That surprises you, doesn't it?' she added, seeing Melissa's startled expression.

'It astonishes me,' she retorted dryly—and it was an understatement. But she was flooded with relief. For it seemed that she had misjudged Ben all over again. She realised how little she really knew of the man she loved so much.

'Well, it's true. I hate to admit it but he only just managed to whip up enough enthusiasm to kiss me goodnight after the dance on Saturday and then he 'made an excuse and left' as the press boys say when they've been investigating naughty goings-on,' Vicki declared, brown eyes dancing with merriment.

Melissa raised an eyebrow. 'What happened to your plans for a midnight swim?' She sounded cool but her heart was thudding and she realised just how much she had hated the thought of her friend in Ben's arms. She would have forgiven him that as she forgave him everything else, but it would have lurked at the back of her mind like a canker in the loveliest of roses to haunt her if he ever held her again.

'Oh, that just fizzled out. No one was keen and Ben decided that the sea was probably too cold as you'd said, murmured something about another time and then asked me where I lived so pointedly that it was obvious that any hopes I might have cherished of naughty goings-on were doomed to disappointment.' Vicki heaved a mock sigh. 'I *did* fancy him, too . . .'

'Well, I certainly thought that he fancied you. Seeing you at the bungalow yesterday . . .'

'I shall never know what goes on in that man's head!' Vicki broke in firmly. 'I told you—I can't make head or tail of him! He turned up out of the blue to take me to lunch and then suggested that we went to his place—to swim and sunbathe and relax, he said. Aha! thought I. Now we're getting down to the nitty-gritty. I haven't lost my sex appeal, after all. He was just taking his time to get round to the idea of bed, unlike most men. More disappointment! He treated me as if I was his maiden aunt—even shut the bedroom door while I changed into a dry bikini after our swim. A most unusual man!'

'Yes,' Melissa said quietly. 'He is . . .'

Despite the terrible anxiety about Neville that still weighed on her spirits, her heart couldn't help lifting at her unsuspecting friend's assurances that Ben had found it as impossible as she had to go to bed with someone else, whatever his original intention might have been. Wanting her, he hadn't been able to take Vicki as a substitute lover, after all.

'I was glad to see you, to be honest,' Vicki swept on. 'Platonic friendships are all very well but *boring*. Give me a man like your Neville any day,' she added with feeling. 'He makes a woman feel like a woman!'

Melissa glanced at the wall clock. 'I have to get back to Theatres.' She rose. 'You won't have much trouble finding another Neville if that's what you want,' she said lightly, smiling at Vicki. 'But Ben Gregorys are few and far between . . .'

Leaving her friend to make what she liked of those parting words, she made her way from the dining-room and along the maze of corridors to the theatre wing.

It was true, she felt, musing over the confident declaration. If a girl could find her happiness with a man like Neville then she could probably take her pick from a dozen men. He was a dear and a charmer but he wasn't an original.

Whereas Ben was a very rare man. He didn't love lightly or easily and he wouldn't cheat, and it seemed that he didn't reach out and take any woman who offered as she had unkindly supposed. Perhaps she had been something special to him, after all. He was certainly special in her life. Melissa doubted if she could ever find another man like him or one who meant so much and always would.

He made *her* feel like a woman, she thought, recalling Vicki's unexpected and surprising criticism. But she knew just how impersonal and distant he could be and how hard it was for a girl to know what he thought and felt about her. She knew just how frustrating it was to want him and to be held firmly at arms' length, too.

He *was* sexy and exciting and capable of a strong and sensual and very potent passion even if Vicki hadn't discovered that ardour in him. He could be tender and thoughtful and sensitive, too. He was strong and sure and straightforward. She loved his dry sense of humour and she admired his reserve and his intelligence and his compassionate dedication to his work.

Having seen the man behind the mask of detached and self-sufficient surgeon, Melissa knew the pride and the passion, the anger and the ardour, the tension and the tenderness that made up the man she loved. She knew that there was a deep-seated need in him for all that she could give him—and that was much more than sexual satisfaction for a sensual man.

Ben had loved and been hurt, humiliated. Proud and sensitive, he was far from ready to love again. It might never happen. He might never ask her to marry him. But every woman in love had her hopes and dreams of that kind of happiness and it seemed that nothing could shatter hers completely.

Loving him, there was no question of not forgiving him. He had only taken what she would have given gladly if he had approached her in desire instead of that cold and implacable and mystifying anger. She belonged to him anyway. He had made her his own for ever on that unforgettable night and she had already found that it was quite impossible to give herself to any other man. Even Neville . . .

Having checked with Cheryl that she should return to her own theatre that afternoon, she was busy when Ben arrived for an afternoon's intensive work on the delayed list. She smiled at him with a warmth that he couldn't mistake and saw his eyes narrow with surprise. But there was no time for private conversation before the first patient was wheeled in from the ante-room.

Melissa was glad that she could slip into her comfortable rôle as theatre nurse as if the events of the past week hadn't turned her world upside down. She was used to his silent concentration on his work, the brusque instructions or requests, the hint of impatience if she was a second late in handing a swab or an instrument, the way his glance slid over her as though she was just another part of essential theatre equipment.

Because of the morning's emergency, it was a longer working day than it should have been for Ben. Having primed his patients for surgery and issued instructions to ward sisters for preparation and fasting and pre-meds, he disliked postponement for more than a few hours. So, having taken a brief break to eat and relax, he came back to work steadily through most of his arranged list until it was done, the duty surgeon taking care of two minor cases in an adjoining theatre.

The anaesthetist was relieved half-way through the afternoon. Various members of the theatre team went off duty at intervals to be replaced by fresh staff. Melissa's own day should have ended at three o'clock but she chose to work on by Ben's side, glad to be busy because she had less time to think and worry about Neville and knowing that Ben was relying on her much more than he would probably admit. They had made a good team from the first.

Cheryl was constantly in touch with the IC Unit and she came immediately with the news when Neville finally came round fully from the anaesthetic, and again when she learned that the usual tests showed no signs of brain damage.

It was the one thing that Melissa had been dreading, the anxiety uppermost in her mind since she had learned that Neville's shocked heart had twice gone into arrest during surgery and that Ben had worked desperately against time to resuscitate him.

For her sake as much as his patient's, he had declared. As though he believed that she pinned all her hopes of happiness on Neville. Did he? Had she been too convincing when she paraded his love and her pretended response with the proud intention of showing that she was indifferent to a man who didn't seem to care at all?

Pride was dangerous. It could cause too much misunderstanding and heartache and get in the way of happiness. Melissa was determined that she wouldn't bother with it again.

She knew that she hadn't been very kind or generous or encouraging earlier in the day and now she regretted it. No doubt Ben felt that she was more concerned with Neville than for their own on-off relationship that didn't seem to know where it was going, she thought wryly.

She set her juniors to the task of tidying the theatre and hurried to waylay Ben as he came out of the surgeons' changing-room. He glanced at her, unsmiling, cool-eyed. Melissa tried not to feel rebuffed.

Her own smile was warm but not very sure. 'We have to talk, Ben. Do you have to rush away this evening? Why don't we have a drink in the Jubilee . . . ?' It was carefully light.

She was always running after him, she thought ruefully. But what was a girl to do when the man she loved was so elusive and so unpredictable, and sometimes so hurtfully distant?

He raised a sardonic eyebrow. 'And set all the tongues wagging? They are busy enough with your affairs at the moment, don't you think?'

'And getting most of it wrong!'

'I wouldn't know. You don't tell me very much about yourself. Or your family.'

She bridled at the cool words with their implied rebuke. 'That isn't fair! I told you I had relatives in the area and it was one of the reasons why I took this job. I might not have said in so many words that Neville and I are cousins, I suppose. Lots of people know it. I assumed you did, too.'

'More than just cousins, surely.' He glanced at his watch, deliberately dismissive. 'No, I don't think we'll have that drink.' He turned away.

Melissa caught at his arm. 'You can't believe that Neville and I—that I *love* Neville!'

He sighed. 'Melissa, I'm tired. I've had enough for one day. Of this place *and* you *and* your complicated love life.'

She flushed. 'It wasn't complicated until you came into it,' she said with sudden spirit.

'That was my mistake. Now I'm getting out of it.'

Her hand tightened on his arm. The indifferent words might echo in her head but her foolish heart refused to believe them. He *couldn't* mean it. He had heard the absurd rumour that she was engaged to Neville. Hurt and angry and confused, he was trying to hurt in revenge.

'But I want you, Ben,' she said quietly.

He shrugged her hand from his arm. The glow in his grey eyes might or might not have been anger. 'Frankly, I don't give a damn,' he said, entirely without emotion, and strode off down the corridor without a backward glance.

CHAPTER TWELVE

MELISSA had a few days' leave owing to her and Matron raised no objection when she asked if she could take them immediately. She knew that Matron and everyone else assumed that she couldn't concentrate on her work while Neville was so ill and that she wanted to spend as much time as she could with him. She saw no reason to correct them and there was a degree of truth in it, anyway.

Everyone except Ben, of course. But it didn't matter what he thought, she told herself proudly. It didn't matter if he knew that she just didn't want to see him or work with him again until she could accept that he had walked out of her personal life just as abruptly as he had invaded it.

She had known that it must happen after that savage lovemaking that he had forced on her. She had been a fool to hope for anything else. She had been worse than a fool to fall so helplessly in love that she hadn't been able to refuse him anything that he wanted. Now she was left with nothing but painful memories and a heart that still loved far too much.

He had only used her rumoured engagement to another man as an excuse to break off their uncertain relationship, she knew. Not that he had needed any excuse to end something that had never really begun. Ben didn't owe her anything, after all. She had no claim on him.

But it might have been a very different story. Melissa was deeply thankful that there were no signs of a possible pregnancy, either as a result of that first whirlwind lovemaking or that final unhappy encounter. At the back of her mind, there had been a faint anxiety.

Seeming not to know that she was a virgin before he took her to bed, Ben seemed to have been equally unaware that she wasn't the type to safeguard against the eventuality of an unwanted pregnancy by taking the contraceptive pill as so many other girls did. She refused to believe that he was the kind of man who had a careless contempt for the possible consequences of his strong sexuality.

Avoiding the theatre wing, she still saw too much of the SSO during those few days of her leave. For he was in and out of the IC Unit and striding about the hospital and zooming in and out of the car park in that distinctive white Mercedes.

Melissa seemed to catch glimpses of him at every turn. Tall, too attractive and as unsmiling as ever as he kept pace with the many demands that were made on a surgeon's time and energies.

But she only saw him from a careful distance. Ben didn't try to get any closer to her even when she knew without a shadow of doubt that he had seen her—sitting with Neville, getting out of a lift, walking along a corridor, talking to colleagues or arriving at St Biddulph's in her small and rather shabby car.

Having been slapped down so hard and so unmistakably by the man, Melissa didn't want to get any closer to him.

It hurt too much.

Such a lot of hurt for so little of her life expended on a man who felt that he'd had enough of love to last him a lifetime. He would probably never marry anyone now, Melissa felt. Just as Vicki had said, he would be the kind of bachelor surgeon who was destined to break a good many hearts without ever risking his own.

But Vicki had been wrong to suppose that he was incapable of very heady passion and Melissa couldn't imagine that he would spend the rest of his life as a celibate. There were too many girls who would find it impossible to resist the enchantment in his smile, the warmth of his charm when he chose to exercise it, the charisma of a very attractive man who had so much more than his looks and physique and strong sexuality to recommend him to a woman.

Julie Hastings, for instance.

She had stepped into Melissa's shoes in Theatres at a moment's notice and seemed to be coping very well with the demands of her new job. She had made more impression on the SSO in a matter of days than Melissa had made in three weeks, too. The grapevine said so—and the grapevine wasn't always wrong.

Apparently, Ben was taking far more notice of his new theatre nurse than he had ever taken of her until that eventful day when she had offered blatant encouragement at a time when he hadn't much cared who comforted and consoled him for the loss of the girl he loved.

Over the first shock and the initial blow to his pride, it seemed that he felt he could afford to be more selective, to look around for a girl who suited him more than herself, Melissa thought bleakly.

Julie seemed to be good for him. He wasn't so grim, so

tense, so hostile towards everybody. He smiled more often and seemed prepared to unbend and make friends. The theatre team were beginning to say nice things about him and were more inclined to agree with Jamie Greaves that there was more to the new SSO than they had first thought.

Melissa preferred to believe that he was merely getting to know and be known, and that Julie had very little to do with his more relaxed attitude, his change of manner. But she admitted that Julie was a very nice girl. She was small and slight and sweet-faced and rather solemn. She took life and love just as seriously as Ben. Melissa couldn't imagine that Julie would be swept into bed without a moment's hesitation or the slightest thought for the consequences even by someone as forceful and as ardent as Ben. But she had thought the same thing about herself, of course.

Thinking of him, tears would well without warning and the pain would begin in her breast. So she tried very hard not to think about him.

Instead, she did her best to concentrate on Neville who needed her so much. He was still very ill but making good progress, thanks to the drugs that helped to speed the healing process and keep infection at bay, and the expert care of the hospital staff.

Like all seriously ill patients, Neville was undemanding and grateful for the smallest service, as physically and emotionally dependent as a child on those who were caring for him. Once he had grasped that Melissa was able to stay with him for long periods in those first critical days, he liked to have her near even when he was drowsy from drugs. Her trained eye and reliable nursing skills made her a welcome asset to the overworked staff of the intensive care unit.

Neville was content as long as he could feel the touch of her hand and sometimes Melissa sat beside his bed for an hour or more while he slept, silent but watchful, thinking thoughts that didn't make her very happy, trying to come to terms with what the future did offer and trying not to mourn for what it didn't hold.

The work of the unit went on around her and Ben came in and went out again and once actually came over to look at Neville's chart and study the monitor and make a brief examination of his patient without a glance or a word for the nurse who sat beside the bed.

Melissa couldn't be sure if it had been the casual indifference of a busy doctor too used to the presence of nurses as he went about his work or the deliberate indifference of a man who had decided to dismiss one particular nurse from his life. She was very sure that he had known her, despite the regulation gown and mask and the cap that concealed her mass of distinctive ash-blonde hair.

Everyone at St Biddulph's knew that she was keeping vigil at Neville's bedside for much of the day, after all. Everyone at St Biddulph's was declaring that he owed his slow but sure progress to her obvious devotion, too.

She *was* devoted to Neville. Sitting with him during those critical post-operative days, studying the fair, good-looking face with its ethereal pallor, watching for the blue eyes to open and know her and respond with the slightest of smiles, Melissa knew that she loved him dearly.

But it was a very different kind of love from the one

that had stormed into her life and taken possession of her heart, swept away her pride as well as her virginity and cost her so much pain. It was a wiser, more lasting love with a true promise of happiness, Melissa decided proudly.

Ben's kind of loving had been such deep and dangerous waters for an untried girl. Neville's kind of loving promised a safer if unexciting harbour for the rest of her life. She would be very foolish if she persisted in clinging to a dream of happiness with Ben when she had the reality of contentment with Neville within her grasp.

People referred to him as her fiancé quite frequently. Melissa didn't correct them. She knew that Neville loved her. She was willing to marry him as soon as he was well.

Four days after the accident, he was transferred from intensive care to Men's Surgical. Melissa was delighted by an almost overnight improvement in his condition but she had seen it happen too many times to be surprised. He was doing well but it would be a long time before he was discharged from hospital.

She was all the more pleased because his transfer to a ward coincided with her own return to Theatres. He wouldn't need her quite so much now and she could rely on Vicki with her warm smile and friendliness and lively sense of humour to speed Neville's convalescence.

As soon as he was settled in a side-ward, still too ill for the hustle and bustle of the main ward, she slipped in to see him before she was due to report for duty.

He was very tired of course. Even the small excitement of being moved from one part of the hospital to another was exhausting for a patient in his condition.

He lay against the pillows, pale and drained, eyes

closed, swathed in the plaster that was helping his crushed ribs to heal, still needing the drainage tube and the drips and the monitor and the cylinder of oxygen with its mask that stood in readiness for any emergency.

Melissa kissed him gently.

Neville opened his eyes, smiled. 'Who is it?' he murmured. 'All nurses look the same. Go and put on a mask so I can recognise you . . .'

Tears welled at that first welcome attempt at light-hearted humour. It was a pleasing sign that he was really on the mend, she felt.

'It's marvellous that you're feeling and looking so much better,' she said, taking his hand to her cheek in an impulsive, loving gesture.

His long fingers curved to stroke her soft cheek. 'You won't have to wheel me down the aisle or carry me over the threshold, I promise . . .'

A little colour stole into Melissa's face. He was well enough now to take notice of the kind of comments that had been passing over his head for the last few days, she realised.

'Oh . . .' she said, rather uncertainly.

There was a flicker of amusement in the very blue eyes. '*Oh*, indeed . . .' It was gently teasing. He searched her face with intent eyes. 'How long have we been engaged? A man likes to know these things . . .'

She smiled at him, warm and tender. 'Just as long as you like,' she said quietly, burning her bridges.

'Time to tell the family then . . .'

'They already know,' she admitted with a slightly rueful smile. 'It was all over the hospital that you're my fiancé and they were bound to hear it. They are so pleased . . . and it's given Aunt Eleanor something else to think about. It's been rather a worrying time for everyone.' It was a quiet statement without any hint of reproach for an accident that no one could have foreseen or done anything to prevent.

'Haven't known . . . much about it—except that you . . . were always there . . .' Neville was tiring, finding it more of an effort to talk. 'Just as it should be . . .'

'Just as it will be,' Melissa assured him promptly. Trained fingers sought the too-rapid pulse. 'Don't talk any more now, darling. Try to sleep. I have to go now, anyway. I'm on duty this morning. But I'll come back to see you again later.'

'What . . . did you call me . . . ?'

Melissa pushed the thick fall of blond hair from his brow and kissed him. 'Darling . . .' she said gently.

Neville smiled. 'Sounds nice.'

Vicki came into the side-ward at that moment with a covered tray. He was due for another injection.

'I hope you aren't exciting my patient,' she said brightly. 'That's *my* job! Unless you have a special dispensation from Matron.'

Melissa laughed as she moved away from the bed towards the open door. 'We *are* engaged,' she declared, stating it as confirmation of the busy grapevine rumour for the very first time. 'Does that count?'

'Just my luck!' Vicki smiled down at Neville with warm brown eyes as she checked the smooth flow of the drip. 'The best-looking man we've had in here for months, too. I thought you were a friend, Melissa!'

Pausing in the doorway, blocking the entry of a man that she was deliberately pretending not to have seen for all his distinction of bronze hair and white coat and tall build, Melissa said lightly, 'Never mind. You can have the SSO. With my blessing.'

'Excuse me, Nurse.'

She stepped out of the way. As their eyes met, she knew that he had heard both that light but meaningful announcement and the rider that she had fully intended for his ears.

'Good morning, Mr Gregory,' she said, very cool, merely polite. 'How have you been managing in Theatres without me?'

He paused and looked down at her without warmth. 'Perfectly well.' He was curt. 'Nurse Hastings has proved to be an excellent substitute.'

Melissa's chin tilted and she looked back at him with a slightly militant sparkle in the dark blue eyes. 'In more ways than one, I hear,' she challenged. It was unwise but irresistible.

Ben's eyes hardened abruptly. 'Entirely to my satisfaction,' he said deliberately.

'Good!' She began to turn away before her hurt betrayed her.

'By the way. I understand that you'll be assisting Mr Savage permanently in future,' he added smoothly.

Checked by the words, Melissa was dismayed, furious. 'Is that your doing?' she demanded coldly.

Ben shrugged. 'A word in the right ear can work wonders,' he said indifferently, not bothering to explain that John Savage had made the request and that he hadn't protested when Cheryl turned to him for comment, believing that it was what Melissa wanted.

'It suits me very well,' Melissa said, cold and hard,

that little core of pain threatening to spread and over-whelm her. She forgot how many times she had already misjudged this man, convinced that he had carried out an earlier threat. 'John Savage is one of the nicest men I know. You're just a bastard—in *and* out of Theatres!'

She turned on her heel and flounced along the corri-dor towards the swing doors of the ward, flaming, not caring if the angry words had carried all the way to Matron's office . . .

Pride prevented Melissa from protesting at the loss of her particular job to Julie Hastings. Pride compelled her to assure Cheryl that it didn't matter to her which surgeon she worked with as long as she was still an 'instrument nurse' who assisted at operations and not a 'dirty nurse' or a 'runner', although both were very necessary members of the theatre team. She had worked too hard to win her position in Theatres to lose it, after all.

It was true that she had a great deal of gynae surgery experience and therefore was possibly more useful to John Savage than to a general surgeon. She wasn't petty enough or conceited enough to suppose that Julie wasn't just as efficient and capable and conscientious as herself and it seemed that Ben had no cause for complaint.

But she had enjoyed working with Ben despite every-thing, and it grieved her that they were no longer together as a team. She felt that she had lost her last contact with him—and heaven knew that he was elusive enough at any time! Now, she seldom saw him at all and they exchanged only the minimum of necessary remarks when they did meet.

She reminded herself firmly that she had promised to

marry Neville and therefore shouldn't want any kind of contact with Ben, now or in the future. But that didn't help her to love him any the less and her longing for him persisted as the days passed and they both continued to pretend that the other didn't exist.

Melissa felt quite sick with jealousy and despair when she saw Julie hanging on his every word and basking in the warmth of the enchanting smile that seemed to be so much in evidence of late.

How could she know that Ben was particularly nice to his new theatre nurse whenever he knew that the old theatre nurse was within earshot?

She liked Julie. She was a thoroughly nice girl, sweet and gentle and eager to please. But she certainly wasn't right for Ben, Melissa thought with a growing anxiety as rumours about their relationship grew thick and fast.

He needed someone who would stand up to him and check that tendency towards arrogance. He needed someone to laugh with him and Julie was just as serious about everything as he tended to be. He needed some-one who could match him for strength and spirit and sensuality. Someone like herself . . .

But she was engaged to Neville. Off duty, she wore the gold signet ring that he had slid on her finger to stand proxy for the diamond solitaire that he had promised to buy for her as soon as he was discharged from hospital.

Looking forward to their wedding and the house they would buy and the family they would have was getting him back on his feet much more quickly than anyone could have anticipated when he was first brought in to Accident and Emergency after being extricated from his crumpled sports car. He was full of plans for the future and full of confidence for their mutual happiness.

Melissa couldn't allow him to suspect that she dreaded the very thought of marrying him at all. Dear though he was, much as she loved him, heart and mind and body shrank from the prospect of spending the rest of her life with him when she ached with every fibre of her being for a very different man.

She knew that she was living a lie and the strain was beginning to tell. She tried not to think about Ben. She tried not to think how much she missed him, how much she loved and needed him. She tried not to think how eager and impatient she would be for the wedding day to dawn if she was going to marry Ben. It wasn't easy.

She lost a little weight. Too many restless and dream-filled nights left the faint smudge of weariness beneath the dark blue eyes and she was paler than she should have been. She was jumpy and on edge, nerves constantly on the stretch, mind and heart constantly on the watch for the smallest sign of softening in Ben's attitude to her. But since her engagement to Neville had become official, he had scarcely spoken to her. He never smiled and didn't seem to want to remember that they had once found a kind of heaven in each other's arms.

Neville's happiness had to come before her own. Particularly when there wasn't the slightest hope of finding it with Ben. She tried to take comfort in the belief that Neville loved and needed her much more than Ben ever would or could . . .

Or did he?'

For as Neville grew stronger and left the side-ward for the spacious open ward and began to take more of an interest in his surroundings and his fellow-patients and the nurses on the ward, he seemed to be less dependent on her for the brightening of his days. Without even looking for it or consciously wishing for it, Melissa began to realise his growing dependence on someone else. She didn't think that he was aware of it as yet.

She was sure that he didn't realise the way his gaze followed Vicki as she moved about the ward attending to the various needs of the patients, smiling and cheerful, not quite flirting but certainly feminine enough to rally the most depressed of men. Nor did he realise that his face brightened at her approach, that his voice took on a new gentleness and warmth and that there was as much affection as gratitude in the way he looked and spoke and smiled at his pretty and very personable nurse.

It was not at all unusual for a patient to fall in love with his nurse during a long stay in hospital, of course. Such feelings seldom survived discharge and the return to the world outside the hospital walls. It was accepted as an occupational hazard by nurses who worked on a male ward. Some were flattered, others merely amused when it happened. But all knew better than to encourage affectionate or amorous advances from a patient.

It seemed that Vicki either didn't know just how much encouragement she offered in the way she smiled at Neville with those warm brown eyes and the way she lingered over any routine chore she had to perform for him—or else she was already too smitten to care.

Melissa remembered that they had always liked each other. She recalled that they had got on very well at that dance just before Neville's car had lost its wheel and spun off the road. She couldn't help feeling that Vicki was much better suited to someone like Neville than herself.

In a few weeks he had made a marvellous recovery. But he was still some way from being really fit again and no definite date had been fixed for the wedding. With all her heart, Melissa hoped it would never take place. With all her heart, she hoped that he was falling seriously in love with Vicki and that her light-hearted and very fickle friend was falling seriously in love with him, too.

It certainly looked that way. But she told herself to be careful that she didn't see things as she wanted them to be rather than the way they were. She mustn't interpret their very warm liking for each other and their obvious rapport as loving just to suit her own hopes and dreams or she might be tempted to do all she could to push them into each other's arms regardless of where their happiness really lay.

Melissa wished she didn't still know so surely exactly where her own happiness could be found.

It hurt too much . . .

CHAPTER THIRTEEN

AFTER an emergency Caesarean to bring reluctant twins into the world, Melissa was rather late in leaving Theatres. With her mind on Neville and Vicki and the suspicion that they were rapidly approaching an emotional crossroads when something would have to be done about an engagement that had never been properly planned, she took a corner much too sharply.

She collided with Ben, tall and muscular with the powerful build of an ex-rugger player. She was winded by the unexpected and quite forceful encounter—and abruptly reminded of another occasion when he had barged into her without apparently seeing her. Although she hadn't known it at the time, that had been the start of the involvement that had brought her so much heartache and humiliation, she thought with sudden bitterness.

'I wish you'd look where you're going!' she flared unfairly.

His hand had sped to her slender waist to steady her rocking frame with automatic concern and courtesy before he saw that it was Melissa. It fell to his side at her tart words. He didn't trust himself enough to let it linger with the need to know again the warmth and softness and sweetness of her flesh, too often in his mind when memories stirred to haunt him and torment him and fill his days and nights with longing.

'You shouldn't cut corners.'

'There's no need to apologise. It must have been my fault,' she said scathingly.

Ben raised an eyebrow, sardonic. 'You had your head filled with romantic notions of happy ever after, I daresay,' he said dryly.

Her chin tilted. 'As it happens—yes!' Not her own—but there was no need to admit that to a man who wasn't interested in what she thought or felt any more.

She moved to walk on as the duty surgeon came out of Theatre Sister's office and glanced at them curiously as he crossed the corridor to the surgeons' changing-room. Unexpectedly, Ben fell into step beside her as though he'd forgotten that he'd been heading the other way when they collided.

Melissa glanced up at him doubtfully. He was taut, unsmiling. A nerve was throbbing in that lean cheek. Her foolish heart wrenched with tender concern for him as she saw the signs of strain about the grey eyes and the sensual mouth. He had been working too hard, too-long hours. He was tired and tense. She wondered if that rumoured relationship with Julie Hastings wasn't very satisfactory for a man who obviously needed the release and the relaxation and the ease of mind and body that sex could give him.

'You look as if you've had a rough day,' she said impulsively.

His mouth tightened. 'Keep your concern for Page. He needs it more than I do.' He was brusque.

Melissa flushed. 'Why are you always so bloody about Neville?' she demanded in sudden indignation. 'You've no reason to dislike him so much! You can't possibly be jealous when you had much more from me than he ever did!'

'A likely story.' Ben had a very vivid memory of her standing at the flat door in the early hours, every line of her lovely body emphasised by the thin robe that had obviously been hastily drawn about her to conceal her nudity.

'True, nevertheless!' Melissa was abruptly aflame with anger as a lurking resentment broke its bounds and swept her beyond pride or caution. 'If you hadn't been in such a hurry to take what you wanted you might have had time to realise that I was a virgin! There's never been any man but you! Before or since!'

Ben stopped short and stared down at her with abruptly narrowed eyes. But he couldn't doubt the bright flame of indignation in those dark blue eyes or fail to realise the ring of sincerity behind the tart and very revealing words.

He shot a glance up and down the corridor. Operating was finished for the day but Theatres was never empty. The duty team was always on stand-by for any emergency. There might never be another opportunity to straighten out the tangle of his involvement with Melissa but a hospital corridor was not an ideal venue.

With sudden resolution, he opened the door of a walk-in linen cupboard and thrust her inside with a strong hand on her shoulder, so swiftly that she didn't have time to realise his intention or to protest.

Closing the door and standing with his back to it so she couldn't escape, he confronted her. 'Say that again!'

Melissa was silent. It wasn't the kind of thing that a girl could repeat in cold blood after all. She had been very angry. Now, she was just tense, heart hammering, not knowing what to make of the glow in those grey eyes and certainly not daring to hope. He was so unpredictable, so unexpected. For weeks he had been behaving as though he was utterly indifferent to her existence. Suddenly, he was throbbing with a new intensity of emotion that transcended mere physical passion.

Ben searched the small, flushed face with intent eyes that slowly and surely warmed as he found what he sought in her soft, tremulous and very appealing shyness. Then he put an arm about her and drew her against him. 'I should have known, of course. But I didn't,' he said quietly.

He didn't kiss her. His embrace was that of friend rather than lover. It held a great deal of regret, of concern, of unexpected tenderness and warmth. But nothing of love, Melissa thought with a pang of dismay and despair.

She could feel the strong beat of his heart against her breast. She could sense the turmoil in him. It was emotional rather than sexual. She didn't want him to rob her of the cherished memories of that glorious night of love with an expressed regret that it had ever happened at all and she knew that it was trembling on his lips. She regretted many things that had ruined their relationship. But she couldn't regret that generous giving for his delight and her own.

'I didn't mean it as a reproach,' she said carefully. 'I wasn't a reluctant virgin. I wanted you too much.' It was very honest.

Ben's arm tightened about her abruptly. 'You were very sweet,' he said gently. 'Warm and wonderful and unforgettable. Just what I needed—and I've missed you. So much.' He sighed and touched his lips to her pale hair. 'It shouldn't have gone so wrong when it was so very right, Melissa.'

Her heart and her body were stirring in response to him and her usually level head didn't seem to care that they were risking the wrath of the powers that be and possible dismissal from their respective jobs with this illicit interlude in a hospital store-room.

She allowed an arm to steal about his neck, allowed her body to hint at melting, allowed her heart to hope just a little in response to those unexpected and very comforting words.

She drew delight and comfort from his very physical presence, the satisfying warmth and strength of his arms about her and his continued need of her for whatever reason. Whatever Ben wanted from her she would give, with a glad heart because she loved him. She had so much to give him. All her love, all her life—if only he wanted it!

She wouldn't be cheating Neville. Because Neville was so near to realising that he didn't really want to marry the 'little cousin' who had become his fiancée more by chance than design. For a little while he had loved her and believed it to be the real thing. But in his heart he was already discovering that someone else was much more important to his lasting happiness.

Melissa raised her face for Ben's kiss. Then, sensing the doubt and hesitation in him, she put both hands to his head and drew it down so she could kiss him, soft and sweet and very warm. It was a seal of forgiveness. It was a declaration of loving if he wanted to accept it as such.

'Friends again . . . ?' It was a soft murmur against his lips.

She saw the smile that she loved begin in his eyes and gradually soften the austere planes of that very attractive face.

'Half a loaf isn't much for a starving man,' he said with unmistakable meaning. He held her more closely to him and Melissa sensed the beginning of desire in his powerful body.

'I'm inclined to think it's more than you deserve,' she retorted, half-tart, half-teasing, holding slightly back from the enchantment in that embrace.

'It is,' he agreed wryly. 'When I think of that day at the beach . . . Oh, Melissa . . .' There was deep shame and remorse and sorrow in the soft sigh of her name.

Instantly, she melted against him. She hadn't meant to remind him of something that they both needed to forget. She smiled into his eyes, kissed him. 'As long as you don't do it again . . .'

'Hand on my heart . . .' Smiling, he suited the action to the words. Then he kissed her, his mouth coming down in sudden, urgent passion to find her own. His hand was so close to her breast as they stood together that it was only natural that it should curve about the soft, warm mound that thrust so temptingly against the thin theatre frock.

His kiss was deep and exciting and his hard body pressed against her own with urgent reminder and sensual promise. Melissa quivered and clung to him, quickening in the ardent embrace that she had missed so much, longed so much to know again.

Until the day she died, she would love this man and

respond to him at a touch, a kiss, the murmur of her name, she knew. No other man could ever fill her with such exquisite longing, promise so much ecstatic delight or sweep her so swiftly and surely towards surrender.

She found the strength of mind from somewhere to draw away from him. Her heart was thumping and she was weak with wanting, her body throbbing and melting before the heat of that mutual flame of soaring passion.

'No . . . no more!' She thrust her hands against his powerful chest to keep him at a reasonably safe distance. 'You make my head spin.' She laughed shakily. 'Like wine . . .'

Ben took her face in both strong hands and looked deep into her eyes with longing. 'Then give me tonight and let us both be drunk with loving,' he said softly. 'We'll make it a night to remember . . .'

Perhaps it was madness. Perhaps she was inviting fresh heartache and humiliation. Perhaps he only wanted from her what any woman could give him. He spoke of loving too lightly—and with unmistakable meaning. It wasn't the kind of loving that she felt for him and needed to know in return. But he wanted *her* when there were so many other women only too eager to embrace him, please him, delight him. There must be more to his desire for her than a basic sexual need. This had to be a new beginning and the promise of a very different ending. He only asked for one night. She would gladly give the whole of her life if it would make him happy . . .

She wore her prettiest frock and brushed her hair till it shone and felt that she looked lovely for him when he arrived at the flat later that evening. She saw the instant admiration, the glow of warm delight in his grey eyes. She liked the hint of restraint in the way he kissed her, so lightly but with so much promise. She still trembled at his touch and knew the eager leaping of impatience for his lovemaking.

Ben took her to an expensive restaurant on the coast road. Newly opened, it had no memories of Neville or anyone else to shadow their evening and she wondered if he had chosen the place for that very reason.

The food was good, the wine excellent and the décor managed to be modern without losing any of its romantic intimacy. Charming and attentive, Ben was an amusing and delightful companion, setting out to please as if he didn't realise that just to be with him on such friendly terms was pleasure enough for Melissa.

It was nice to see another side to the man she loved. This was their first proper date, she realised. From the beginning their relationship had been turbulent, and there hadn't been time for the usual preliminaries of a normal courtship. He had rushed her into bed as though it was the only thing that mattered. Certainly it had been a primary need with him at the time. She felt that he meant everything to be different the second time around and she was warmed, reassured, encouraged to hope.

Ben poured the last of the wine into their glasses and smiled at her across the small table.

Like a lover, Melissa thought, her heart stirring in response to the very attractive man who meant all the world to her. If only he loved her in the true sense of the word. As she loved him! If only he needed her as she needed him—with heart and soul as much as body.

But surely there was the tenderness of loving in the

way he looked, the way he reached for her hand and took it to his lips to press a kiss into the palm in a lover's gesture. Surely there was much more than sexual longing in the pressure of his mouth and the smile that lurked in the deep-set grey eyes.

'Where do we go from here, Melissa?' he asked quietly.

She misunderstood him. 'Your place or mine, do you mean? I don't mind.' The quick, warm words and the look in her eyes conveyed her readiness to lie in his arms all night in the middle of Baymouth market square if he should wish it, if it would please him.

Ben was humbled by the warmth and generosity and goodness of this girl's heart. It was still her own, too, he felt. Despite that engagement to another man. With time and patience and a more sensitive handling of her tender and untried emotions, it might eventually belong to him.

He had tried very hard to believe that he wanted Melissa's happiness even at the expense of his own. He loved her enough for that, he had told himself firmly. He must accept that she cared for someone else, meant to marry her cousin at the first opportunity. He must keep out of her life and make it easier for her to forget the feelings that he had evoked in her and which still leaped to life too easily.

But now he knew that he only wanted her happiness as long as it lay with him. He believed that it did. He merely had to convince Melissa that it was so.

'That isn't what I meant,' he said gently. 'But I think the bungalow, don't you? We have to lay a ghost.' She looked slightly startled. He smiled and rose to his feet, held out his hand to her with a sudden glow in his eyes. 'Oh, Melissa,' he said, very soft, very urgent. 'I want you all over again . . .'

The words with their throbbing sexuality, the fire in his eyes, quickened her to swift and eager response. She smiled at him, tremulous, lovelier than she knew.

In the car, he kissed her, a brief promise of delight to come. Sitting beside him as he drove the short distance to Spelby and the bungalow, she was tingling, a melting warmth stealing in her veins, an ache of longing in her loins and her breasts throbbing to know his sensual caresses and the physical, exciting contact with his warm, strong flesh. It was too long since he had held her and taken her with him to the soaring heights of the heaven that man and woman could find in each other's arms.

She hadn't minded that frank admission of his need for her. She felt it herself and knew that it was an important part of their relationship. But only a part of all that they were to each other, her heart insisted. Ben might not be ready to recognise or admit that he loved her. But she was sure that he did. She could wait until he felt that the moment was right for a final and lasting commitment. In the meantime, she just couldn't refuse him anything . . .

Yet she hesitated on the wooden verandah of the bungalow, the memory of his urgent and uncaring love-making rushing into her mind. She might have forgiven. She was finding that it wasn't so easy to forget.

She turned to look across the dunes to the cliffs, sombre in the fading twilight. She gripped the wooden rail with both hands, tense and uncertain and apprehensive. Could she lie with him on that same bed, in that same room, and not remember? Would memories turn her frigid and rigid in his arms all over again? She knew instinctively that this night was a turning point in both their lives. What if she disappointed Ben with a lack of response that he construed as lack of loving?

He came to stand behind her and enfold her in his arms, resting his cheek on her soft hair, drawing her close against him. Melissa could feel the thud of his heart and sense the tension and the uncertainty in him. But his arms were strong and sure and very tender and she longed to keep them about her for ever.

She loved him so much.

She wondered why it was so impossible to tell him, quietly and without drama, meaning it with all her heart.

'Shall I take you home?' he asked softly.

Melissa liked his swift understanding, his sensitivity. But she suddenly realised what he had meant by saying that they had a ghost to lay. It was true. He was wiser than herself. Ben knew that if he didn't make love to her in very different fashion in these very same surroundings, the memory of that former lovemaking would always haunt them both and eventually destroy their delight in each other.

'No . . .' Melissa leaned back against him, relaxing. Loving him, she must trust him. Loving him, she mustn't hurt him with reluctance.

His lips were warm on her neck, nuzzling. His breath sighed softly through her hair. He said her name and that was a sigh, too.

She took his hands and drew them to her breasts in a gesture of loving and very willing surrender.

He drew in his breath sharply.

Melissa turned slightly to smile at him, with love, with tenderness, with her heart in her eyes.

'Must you marry Neville?' he said abruptly.

She shook her head. 'I don't think I could,' she admitted with the instinctive, impulsive candour that was so unconsciously endearing.

'Could you marry me?'

She turned completely in his arms to look at him with wide, startled eyes. Her heart was floundering like a wild thing in her astonished, unbelieving breast.

'Are you asking?' she said doubtfully, a little shyly, not daring to believe that he could mean the astonishing and unexpected proposal.

He laughed softly. 'Yes, I'm asking.' He tilted her small, sweet face with a light hand beneath her chin and kissed her, with love.

She was suddenly illumined with a radiant happiness that made her very lovely in his eyes. 'Oh, Ben . . .' Her arms went up and about his neck in an instant and she kissed him back on a tumult of relief and thanksgiving and glad, soaring delight.

'Are you answering?' he said, teasing. 'I don't know if that's yes or no!'

Melissa smiled, tremulous, very much in love and just beginning to believe that perhaps, after all, despite everything, he really did love her too. 'I think it's *why*!'

He smiled down at her, very warm. 'Because I love you,' he said simply. 'Can you think of a better reason?'

Then he kissed her, long and lingering. And if there was the least doubt in her heart about the truth and the sincerity of his words, it fled before the kiss that held so much more than physical, short-lived passion in its tender warmth—a promise of real and lasting happiness.

Later, lying in his arms, content and fulfilled and glowing, very sure that her eager and loving response had delighted and satisfied him completely, Melissa was glad that Ben had told her that he loved her and wanted to marry her before instead of after the power and the glory of that splendid lovemaking which had not only laid a ghost but also a foundation on which to build the future.

It was so much more convincing . . .